SWEET TEXAS *Fire*

NICOLE FLOCKTON

To Delene!
Enjoy the Texas Fire!
Best Wishes
Nicole Flockton

Crimson Romance
New York London Toronto Sydney New Delhi

CRIMSON
ROMANCE
Crimson Romance
An Imprint of Simon & Schuster, Inc.
1230 Avenue of the Americas
New York, NY 10020

ISBN 978-1-4405-9552-3
ISBN 978-1-4405-9551-6 (ebook)

To Marcy Schuler – you were taken from us too soon. Thank you for your cheerleading and support of the romance community. I'm going to miss you and your flaming marshmallow.

Chapter 1

Gage Cooper drummed his fingers on the armrest as the plane taxied toward the gate. He wasn't used to the slow crawl of a commercial flight. Unfortunately, his jet was undergoing some routine maintenance. He'd needed to get back to Houston in a timely matter and couldn't wait the extra eight hours it would take for his plane to be ready.

At least he was able to get a ticket in first class at the last minute.

"Is there anything I can get you once we finish taxiing, Mr. Cooper?" The sultry voice of the flight attendant, who'd been trying her best to flirt with him the whole flight, pulled his attention from his internal thoughts.

He knew the attendant wasn't inquiring whether he wanted some peanuts for the walk down the tunnel to the terminal. On any other given day, he might be tempted to take her up on the offer. Right at this moment, he had business hassles popping up every three minutes.

"Thank you, but no, I'm fine." He turned to look out the window, relieved to see the plane pulling up to the gate. He undid his seat belt before the plane stopped. He wanted to be first in line to collect his luggage and then get into a cab.

While another flight attendant welcomed everyone to Houston, Gage was reaching into the overhead locker to take out his carry-on and laptop bag. As he waited for them to open the doors, he grabbed his phone out of his pocket and checked his e-mails. Hopefully, no more drama had cropped up while he'd been in the air from Midland to Houston. Quickly thumbing through his in-box, nothing seemed like it needed his immediate attention.

Relief swept through him. He'd spent the last month dealing with the unenviable task of reducing the output on some of his rigs due to the downturn in oil prices. Not to mention the petty environmental issues he'd had thrust on him over the last few months as well by his nemesis, Charlotte Wilkinson. He'd never had problems in the past with the environmental agency he'd always worked with. That was, until Charlotte began working for Gold Star Eco and started investigating the deals his company worked on. So what if the other guy hadn't been anal about compliance issues. Charlotte focused all her attention on his company now and made the process a nightmare. He was sure she'd found the most obscure plant in the world that needed protecting on his site in Midland. Didn't she know how much money he would lose if he had to move his rig even one foot from the original plan? He knew he needed to care about the environment, but her almost tyrannical approach to protecting something no one had heard of made him want to pull his hair out.

And now she owned the piece of land he'd thought was his.

Finally, the doors opened and he stalked out of the plane, giving the flight attendants a cursory nod. Making his way down the tunnel, he ignored the constant beeping of his phone from more e-mails coming in. He almost gave in to the temptation to turn it off again. He needed to keep his mind clear so he could formulate his plan to confront Charlotte and demand to know what spell she'd cast over his father.

His phone rang as he climbed into a cab after waiting for what seemed like forever to get his luggage. He pulled the device from his pocket, glancing at the screen to see his brother's name.

"Hey, Gray. What's up?"

"I still don't control Guac Olé."

Gage suppressed a sigh. If he'd had it tough over the last month since the reading of his father's will, Grayson had it worse, expecting to inherit controlling share of the company he'd loved as much as his father had. His older brother ended up with nothing but a strawberry charm.

"And I don't have the land I could do with right now, seeing as the price of oil has tanked in the last few months." What Gage did have was a key and twenty five percent of a company he didn't want.

"What was the old man thinking?" Grayson lamented. "He knew what we expected to receive. Hell, he told me not two weeks before he died that everything was sorted out and that all of us would be happy with the contents of his will."

"I know. Have you spoken to Gavin? Has he worked out what the glasses he inherited mean?"

"Don't know, he's been somewhat occupied with other things. If he did work it out, he hasn't mentioned anything to me. What about the key? Any luck there?"

"No. The key is still a mystery to me."

Gage had spent some of the time while he was away visiting his rigs Googling images of keys to see if he could find something that matched the one his father had left him. He gave up when his vision started going blurry after the tenth page. Nothing seemed to match the elaborately ornate key with its thin, round blade and two-pronged tip. The key looked like it belonged in a fairy tale rather than in his possession. He could only assume it was custom-made to fit a unique lock.

He had no idea where to start looking for the lock it would fit into. There had to be something Dad wanted him to find. But what that thing was, he had no idea.

One thing he did know—he really didn't want to have this conversation in a cab. "I've got to go, Gray. I'll give you a call later on tonight."

"Wait. I actually wanted to find out if you were free to come into the office tomorrow."

"Not sure. It's not like it's down the road for me. I'll have to check my schedule. I don't know what Dana's organized for me. It's my first full day back in the office after being out for a month. What time were you thinking?"

"Why don't we make it for drinks and then dinner? That way you can try to clear as much as possible off your desk and drive down to Sweet Ridge. Let me know if that works."

"Okay, I'll send you a text once I know for sure."

"Great. See you, Gage."

"Bye, Gray."

Gage disconnected the call. He rested against the headrest and closed his eyes. He was still trying to come to terms with his father's death. He'd left Houston the day after the meeting with Dad's lawyer. The only emotion he'd felt then was anger. And he'd had plenty of time over the last month for the anger to simmer below the surface.

The cab's slowing pulled him from his reverie. There was the familiar sight of his building just beyond the traffic lights.

Home sweet home.

More like a place to rest his head between trips. The condo could never be called a home. He'd worked in so many different locations that he'd lost the sense of what a home should be. A place where everything was happy, like the family sitcoms he'd watched as a teenager. Oh, the house he'd grown up in had been a home, when their mother had been alive. Even though, with the hindsight of an adult, he now recognized the tension between his parents.

Grayson reached into his pocket and pulled out his wallet as the cab came to a halt. He passed the driver enough cash for the fare and a tip, got out of the car, and walked into the foyer of his condo's building, nodded to the doorman, and made his way to the bank of elevators.

Screw thinking about happy families. He needed to focus on his upcoming meeting. He had to make sure he had all the facts … well, what he thought were the facts.

It wasn't going to be a pleasant meeting. He'd never met Charlotte Wilkinson. With the way she sounded on the phone with her hoity-toity British accent, she was probably a scorned middle-aged woman. No a doubt divorcée who hated all men. It was the only explanation he could come up with for the way she expected his company to kowtow to the petty environmental issues she always highlighted in her e-mails and reports to him.

Now he had another reason to be angry with her. What had she done to Dad to convince him to bequeath the house and surrounding ten acres of land outside of Sweet Ridge to her? Land he knew held a decent oil deposit beneath its surface. Had she blackmailed him? Claimed to be a long-lost daughter? Or worse, had she seduced his father? He shuddered at the thought. He hoped his father was smarter than getting sucked in by a woman. Or women, considering the contents of his will.

He'd started visiting Sweet Ridge, Texas, in the months prior to his father's death to try to mend their broken relationship. They'd talked about the past, sorted through some of the mistakes he'd made. There had still been more he'd wanted to say to Dad. He'd thought they'd reached an understanding. They'd even discussed Dad leaving the land to Gage.

Did Dad still not trust him?

He ran a successful business. He'd obtained his college degree while working his ass off doing the hard work on oil rigs in places no one would want to go to.

He'd worked for everything he had. His bank account was probably as substantial, if not more, as his father's had been. Hadn't he proved to Dad he wasn't that kid anymore? The one who'd acted impulsively without thinking about the consequences. The kid who believed the world owed him because of his prowess on the football field.

He'd changed, and it burned him that Dad didn't think he deserved the land. He'd told Dad what he planned to do with it. How the profits from pulling the black gold out of the ground would be more than he'd ever make from guacamole—even though the guacamole plant had provided Dad and his family with a very good lifestyle. Dad had seemed excited.

Now Gage knew it had been an act and Dad never planned on leaving him the land at all.

The land had been the first piece of property their father had bought, but for some reason he'd never lived in the house on the property. The family hadn't even gone there for the odd weekend away, like a family fun mini-vacation. Still, the land abutted a stretch of bush that was great for hunting deer, so before Gage had left for college, he'd spent a weekend there with his football buddies. One last hurrah before they all headed off to college, all with dreams of making the big time.

No. He wasn't going to think about that. How he'd been so arrogant and confident. How he hadn't given any thought to what going to college on a full football scholarship really meant. How it didn't matter if you were the star player on the team.

You break the rules, you're out.

His phone buzzed with the reminder that his meeting was going to take place in thirty minutes. He needed to get his head in the game. No way was he going to let Charlotte cause any more delays on his oil fields. And he was going to get back the land that was rightfully his.

No matter what it took.

Chapter 2

Charlotte Wilkinson straightened the pile of files on the right-hand corner of her desk. *A tidy desk equaled a tidy mind*, her father's edict floated through her subconscious. She needed to be focused for the upcoming meeting with Gage Cooper.

She'd developed a picture of him, the owner of a successful oil company, in her mind. He wore a white leisure suit with cowboy boots, a big cowboy hat covering his gray hair, and he had a cigar perched in the corner of his mouth. Gage Cooper no doubt looked a lot like Colonel Sanders.

And she'd have to control the urge to bust out laughing if he did look like the king of fried chicken. She had no idea why he'd called the meeting today. All their previous interactions had been through e-mail and heated phone calls. And on a couple of those phone calls she'd had to advise him that if he yelled at her one more time, she'd hang up. There was no way he was going to talk her into backing down from protecting the land around his oil fields.

A knock sounded on her door. "Yes," she called out.

The company's office assistant opened the door. "There's a Mr. Gage Cooper here to see you." Meredith's eyebrows waggled when she said Gage's name.

Charlotte rolled her eyes and smiled. "Show him in. Thanks, Meredith."

"You can go right in now, Mr. Cooper," Meredith all but simpered, and Charlotte couldn't help but wonder what Gage thought of Meredith's attempt at flirting. If he was like most males hitting their late fifties, he would lap up the attention.

Charlotte took a deep breath, the better to control any threat of laughter when she clapped eyes on Gage Cooper for the first time.

"Ms. Wilkinson, thank you for seeing me today," he drawled in a Texan accent.

She looked up from the map she grabbed so she would look busy when Gage walked into her office. Her mouth dropped open. She couldn't help it. Colonel Sanders would've been a much better option to deal with than the man standing in front of her.

Oh shit.

Gage Cooper couldn't be more than a couple of years older than her. How could a man who looked barely thirty be the owner of a successful oil company? Why, oh why, couldn't he have a beer gut instead of a flat stomach, which, in all likelihood, sported a six-pack—and not of the beer variety. No receding hairline hidden underneath a cowboy hat, either. There was no cowboy hat in sight. He had a full head of dark brown hair that curled slightly over his ears. The five o'clock shadow on his face enhanced his high cheekbones, and his lips, full and no doubt tempting when he stretched them into a smile. At present they were pulled in a straight line, like he was annoyed at what he saw.

Indignation rose within her. She wasn't going to be judged because she was following protocol on ensuring the environment was protected.

Taking the bull by the horns, she stood and walked around her desk, holding out her hand. "Good afternoon, Mr. Cooper. It's a pleasure to finally meet you."

Gage looked at her outstretched hand and then back at her face—dear God, he wouldn't leave her hanging, like the loser kid who held her hand up to the star football player to get a high-five, only to be ignored, would he? A second later her hand was engulfed by his large, warm one. He gripped her hand tightly before releasing it quickly and giving his hand a jiggle before placing it in his pants pocket. If her own hand hadn't been pulsating with pinpricking sensations, she'd take it as a personal slight.

"Please take a seat." She indicated one of her guest chairs before rounding her desk and sitting in her own chair. "I have to say I was a little surprised at your request for a meeting, Mr. Cooper. Especially since our main interactions have been via the phone or e-mail."

He leaned forward; she sat back a little in her chair.

"Gage, please. I think we've had enough discussions for you to call me by my first name. And I thought it was time we met face-to-face. It's a much better way to discuss business, don't you think? You have an intriguing accent, Charlotte. Is it British?"

"Australian. But you're not the first person to mistake me for being British."

"My apologies."

She inclined her head to accept his apology and waited for him to continue. His own accent was smooth and sexy. It could easily make her forget that the man sitting in front of her had been rude and obnoxious, when she had only been doing her job. She understood the need to get the oil from the ground, but there was no need for him not to protect the surrounding environment. He told her on many occasions he liked to think he was doing things the correct way. To a certain extent he was, but she could make him do a better job.

The silence stretched between them. It almost looked like Gage was testing her. But she'd grown up with three brothers. She had plenty of patience and fortitude when dealing with the way a male mind worked. However, she didn't intend to spend the rest of her day in a Mexican standoff with this man.

"How'd you do it?" he asked, as she was about to open her mouth and ask him exactly why he was in her office.

"How did I do what?"

"Did you sleep with him to get it?"

What the hell? Get what? And to suggest that she'd slept with somebody to achieve it was the most insulting thing Gage Cooper could say.

Anger bubbled inside, ready to burst out and fry the rude man standing in front of her.

Wait. Don't fly off the handle. Even though he's being a complete asshole, he's a client.

"I really have no idea what you're talking about. How about you explain to me what it is you think I've done? If it's work-related, I'll have you know that I've never slept with anyone to get anything. Any promotion or job opportunity I've achieved has been through hard work."

Gage stood up to lean over the table, so she stood, as well. No way was she going to let him feel like he could threaten or intimidate her.

"What I'm talking about is the piece of land you inherited."

Immediately, she sat down. She was still coming to terms with the fact that she owned a piece of Texas property. She had no idea what she planned to do about it and she had pushed it to the back of her mind to deal with at a later date. Looked like *a later date* was now.

"How do you know about the land?"

"I know because the land belonged to my father, Jack Cooper. And that land is rightfully mine."

But Jack Cooper was a true gentleman, nothing like this man in her office. Could she even trust this was the truth?

Charlotte crossed her arms across her chest. "I think you'd better explain yourself."

"I thought I already did."

"No, you made a lot of insinuations without giving me any proof that what you say is true. Am I just to take your word that you're Jack Cooper's son?"

She waited while Gage pulled out his wallet. He opened it up and laid it on her desk.

"There's all the proof you need."

Keeping her eye on Gage, she reached out and picked up the item. The leather was soft under her touch and warm from residing in his pants pocket. She glanced down—yep, the proof was right there in her hands. In the small plastic pocket sat a picture of four men. In the middle stood Jack Cooper surrounded by, Charlotte assumed, his sons, with Gage standing at the far left of the group. Looking at Gage now and the Gage in the picture, it wasn't taken that long ago. One brother was dressed in a suit and tie; Gage and his other brother wore jeans and western shirts. Even though he smiled, it didn't reach his eyes. He appeared detached, almost uncomfortable to be in the picture.

Why?

Never in a million years would she connect Jack Cooper with Gage Cooper, the owner of one of Houston's most successful oil companies. She recalled from her conversations with Jack that he owned a company that made guacamole. As far removed from oil as Texas was from her home country of Australia.

"Okay, so, yes, you're Jack's son. As to why he left me the land and not you, that's a question I can't answer."

"Oh come on, I know Dad. He must have had a reason for changing his mind. He told me that the land was mine. He told my brother Grayson two weeks before he died that his will was in order. Everyone would be happy, Dad assured him. Well, I'm not happy. I want to know what you did for him to change his will. The same will that named you as the new owner of a piece of land near the town of Sweet Ridge."

Charlotte didn't know what to say. She had no idea why Jack Cooper decided to bequeath her the piece of land.

"Look, I was as surprised as you were when I heard from the lawyer that I now own a piece of Texas real estate."

"Is that right?"

"Yes, as a matter of fact, it is."

A frustrated sigh reached her ears. "How did you meet my dad?"

"As you know, I'm not from around here."

"Yes, I believe we established that earlier. You know, the British versus Australian thing."

"There's no need to be sarcastic. Anyway, while I'm here I've been taking weekend trips to see some of Texas. I came across Sweet Ridge as I was driving to the Gulf and decided to stop for some lunch. I was sitting by myself when your father came up and sat with me." Her mouth stretched into a soft smile. Jack Cooper was an outrageous flirt who reminded her of her favorite uncle, who had died when she was a teenager. Jack made her laugh, and she found that she'd made another couple of trips down just to visit with him. She'd have gone to his funeral, too, if she'd known about his death.

"I'm sorry for your loss, Gage. Until I got the letter from the lawyer, I didn't even know your father had died. I liked Jack and will miss him. The time we shared together will always be a wonderful memory of my time in Texas."

"Well, ain't that sweet," Gage drawled.

It was Charlotte's turn to blow out a frustrated breath. "I really don't like your tone. Your question about my friendship with your father has turned something wonderful, something that meant a lot to me, into something tawdry. You have no right to do that, and if that's the only reason you came to see me, I suggest you leave."

"I'm not leaving yet, Red."

Charlotte rolled her eyes at the reference to her hair color. "Original nickname there, *Cowboy*. But I'm serious—if all you've come here to do is suggest that I have the morals of a whore and seduced Jack into leaving me the land, then I have nothing more to say to you." She tilted her head to the left. "The door is there. I'd appreciate it if you don't slam it on the way out."

"You still haven't given me a definitive answer to my question about why Dad left that piece of land to you," Gage responded as he crossed his arms over his chest, stretching his shirt across his tightly muscled torso.

Damn, he was good-looking. Pity he was such an asshole.

If she'd encountered Gage any other time in a bar or at a party, and the conversation between them didn't suggest she was a whore, she might play with the idea of pursuing a fling with him. However, her tenure in Texas was ending soon, and it would be impractical to pursue anything resembling a relationship.

"I don't know what else to say. I told you I don't know why Jack left me the land. I haven't even gone to see it yet."

"Why not? From what you said earlier, you like Sweet Ridge."

It was true; she liked visiting the small town. But she couldn't bring herself to see what Jack had left her. She knew she would fall in love with it, and it would be the worst thing she could do. When she'd taken on this role, she never thought she'd fall in love with living in Texas.

"Yes, I like Sweet Ridge. I've just been busy so I haven't been able to go."

Gage closed the distance between them, and Charlotte stood up again. "Somehow I think there's more to this story than you're letting on."

"And your suspicious mind is getting tiring, Gage. I don't know how many times I have to say this, but your dad and I were friends. Nothing more. We shared a few lunches together. I told him all about this pain-in-the-ass oilman I had to deal with. And if you need clarification, that pain-in-the-ass oilman is you."

Gage laughed and it changed his whole persona. His eyes lit up, and fine laugh lines appeared around his eyes and mouth, making him even more attractive than when he scowled at her.

"I'm sure Dad would've loved hearing me referred to that way." His eyes dimmed and his mouth firmed. "It pretty much sums up what he thought of me."

"He mentioned to me he had three sons. But he didn't elaborate on what you all did. And I never mentioned your name when we talked. He did tell me that first lunch about how proud he was of all that his sons had achieved in their lives. I'm guessing your other brothers work at the guacamole company?"

If her comment about Jack surprised Gage, he gave nothing away. "No, only Grayson works for the company, and that is another story, too. Gavin is a vet in Sweet Ridge."

"Right." An awkwardness that hadn't been in the room before fell between them. For a first meeting between two business colleagues, the conversation had veered into personal territory.

Gage was within touching distance. The look in his eyes suggested he was aware of the close proximity between them. Mesmerized, she watched as his hand reached out and touched her cheek.

"So tell me, Red, what did you and Dad talk about over lunch if it wasn't his three sons?"

Her cheek burned under the simple touch of his finger. Her ability to speak was lost. She should slap his hand away. She needed to slap his hand away.

"Will you stop touching me?" she whispered. Any control of the situation she might have achieved was lost in the space of five words.

"I don't know if I want to," Gage murmured as his hand spread to cup her cheek. "What is it about you that enamored my father so much?"

Her breath caught when his fingers slipped into her hair, pulling at the strands. "Was it your beautiful red hair? Or maybe it was your mouth. Did you kiss him, Charlotte? Or did you do something else with your mouth that pleased him?"

This time she gasped and pulled away from his hold, cringing as her hair caught between his fingers. "Get out of my office, Gage Cooper, and don't come back."

He didn't move. He just studied her.

Redheads had a reputation for having a temper, but usually Charlotte never had a problem with controlling her anger. However, Gage's suggestion blew her control out the window. If he didn't move in the next five seconds, she was going to pick up her stapler and throw it at him. Damn the consequences of her actions. She wanted him out.

As if he could see the intent in her eyes, Gage headed toward the door, turning to face her again. "This isn't over, Charlotte. Make a note—I will be back."

Chapter 3

Gage walked into the Silver Spurs, Sweet Ridge's honky-tonk bar, and looked around for his brothers. A country ballad blared out from the jukebox in the corner. The main room was surprisingly crowded for a Thursday night. He'd told Grayson he'd be able to make it down late in the afternoon, so he had plans to spend Friday in town, as well. He needed to connect more with his brothers. Before he'd left for college and fucked up his potential football career, they'd all been close.

He also wanted to take the time to look over the land that Charlotte now owned. Oh, he wouldn't trespass on the property. He'd walk the perimeter. He knew from an old survey report there was oil on the land. He didn't know the size of the pocket, but he was hopeful it was a decent one.

If Charlotte knew about the oil pocket, she'd make sure she'd do everything in her power to put a caveat over the land so the oil could never be drilled.

"Gage, over here!"

He looked to the left and spotted the table where Grayson sat, still dressed for the office sans tie. Ties weren't allowed in the Silver Spurs; if someone walked in with a tie on and a waitress spied him, she'd whip out her scissors and cut it off before they had time to say it was made from Italian silk. They didn't care if it was silk or paper. Rules were rules. The array of cut-off ties hanging from the roof and around the walls showed how ruthless the waitresses in the bar could be. Gage rarely wore a tie, so he never had to worry about being made the center of attention.

Gage weaved through the tables, smiling at people he knew as he passed.

"Hey, man." He sat down and picked up the bottle of beer the waitress just placed on the table. Grayson was nothing if not organized.

"Hey, glad you could make it." Grayson raised his gin and tonic in a salute.

"It's good to see you. How's business?"

"Don't ask. It hasn't changed much."

"And the new owner?"

Grayson's face tightened. Gage had a feeling his older brother wouldn't have many nice things to say about the new fifty percent owner of Guac Olé. "She's around somewhere. I haven't tried to have too much to do with her."

"Isn't that a bit difficult? Doesn't she want to take up her place on the executive floor?"

"Nah, she's happy down on the floor working the conveyor lines. Why she does is beyond me. She could be sitting pretty in a corner office, painting her nails."

Gage busted out laughing. "Stop being an arrogant stuffed suit. No wonder she doesn't want anything to do with you if you think she's got nothing but avocado skin for brains."

Grayson rolled his eyes at the weak attempt at humor. "Stick to the oil fields and stop making lame avocado jokes."

"So, where's Gavin?"

"He said he would be here. He's got news for you."

A glint entered Grayson's eyes, and it immediately put Gage on high alert. "Has he found out what the glasses mean?"

Grayson made a zip-closing motion across his lips.

"Fine, I'll wait."

He didn't have to wait long. Seconds later Gage heard the gentle metallic *clang* of Merle's collar. He turned in his chair to greet his other brother and his dog.

"Hey, Gavin, how's it going?"

Gavin clapped Gage on the back. "I'm fantastic, man."

As Gavin took his seat, he, too, picked up his bottle of beer the waitress had placed on the table during their greeting.

There was definitely something different about his oldest brother, but he couldn't put his finger on what it was exactly. The hair was the same. He hadn't grown a moustache. There were no lines of tension around his mouth or eyes that Gage knew showed on his own face and he could see on Grayson's. In fact, Gavin looked happy. Very happy.

"What's got into you, Gavin?"

Grayson spat out his drink on a laugh. "More like what *he's* got into."

Gavin punched Grayson on the arm. There was no malice in the action, just a typical brother-versus-brother play fight. He watched the byplay and felt left out again. The way he'd been feeling the last few years.

"Why do I get the feeling I'm missing something really big and important here?" he asked. "And why are you so damn happy, Gavin? When I left a month ago, you were as pissed off with Dad and the world as I was. What happened?"

"Love happened," Gavin responded, a goofy grin breaking out over his face.

"What the fuck?" Gage shook his head, sure he'd misheard what Gavin had said. "Love?"

"Yep, I'm in love, man, and it feels so good. You oughta try it."

"Wait. Are you telling me that in the month since we were last together, you've fallen in love?"

"That's a fact, Jack!" Gavin quoted an iconic line from the movie *Stripes*. Dad used to make all his sons quote it back to him when Dad was giving them what he called a Jack Cooper Life Rule.

"So, who is this lucky lady? Do I know her?"

For the first time since he'd walked into the bar, Gavin looked a little uncomfortable. "Yeah, you know her. In fact, you could say we all know her."

Gage ran through the names of the girls they all knew. None of them seemed the type to suit Gavin. But hell, after this last month, anything could happen.

"I'm drawing a blank. How about you put me out of my misery and just tell me who this *love of your life* is."

"Macy Young."

Gage slammed his beer bottle on the table. "The same Macy Young who inherited the house from Dad? The Macy who freaked out when you kissed her not that long ago?"

Gavin laughed. "One and the same."

"You're shitting me, aren't you? You took my advice, didn't you? This is all a game to get your hands on the house."

It was the only thing that made sense. Macy and Gavin had always been rivals. But Gavin had apparently forgiven and forgotten everything Macy had done, and now everything was wonderful between them.

"Nope, I'm not wired that way," Gavin replied. "I'm one hundred percent in love with her and she's in love with me. The house is an added bonus."

Gage raised his eyebrow in a silent question at Grayson, who nodded. So, it was the truth.

For a moment he didn't know what to say. He studied Gavin again. He really did look happy, and well, if his brother was happy, who was he to burst his love bubble?

Gage leaned over the table and slapped Gavin on the back. "Congratulations, man."

"Thanks, Gage, and I am. We've all grown up and changed. Even you."

Instead of answering Gavin, he nodded and gulped down some more beer.

"Now that we've got this out of the way, can we talk about why I wanted to meet with you both?" Grayson asked.

"Absolutely. I'm guessing this has to do with Guac Olé and our shares in the company?" Gavin replied.

"Yep, it does."

Gage sat back and took a long swallow of his beer. He didn't want anything to do with the family business. He had his own business he needed to worry about. Not to mention Charlotte Wilkinson.

Damn, but she wasn't what he expected her to look like. She was no middle-aged divorcée. She was probably a couple of years younger than him, her hair a gorgeous shade of auburn, her eyes a clear green that misted over when she got angry. Her body filled her out her smart business suit nicely. He wouldn't mind getting a look at what was underneath that suit. Was she a cotton or lace type of girl?

Whoa. No way.

He couldn't believe the trail his thoughts had meandered onto. She might have cast a spell over Dad, but she wasn't going to cast one over him.

A slap to the back of the head brought his attention back to the Silver Spurs. The sound of the country music blaring from the jukebox, people laughing and talking permeated his consciousness.

"What the f—"

"Language, little brother," Grayson mocked him.

Gage flipped him the bird and took another swallow from his beer. As he set the bottle down he became aware of the silence from the two men sitting in front of him.

"What?" he asked

"Did you hear a word of what I was talking about?" Grayson asked.

Gage scraped a hand down his face. "Sorry, man, I didn't. My mind drifted to a meeting I had yesterday. What did you say?"

Gage withstood the scrutiny from his brothers. Neither one had any idea of the pressure he was currently under with the way the market had dropped out of the oil industry. Over the last month he'd had to lay off people. He hated letting good, hardworking people go. He had also slowed production on some of his rigs. He didn't want to close any down outright, but that could be the next step if the price didn't pick up. He had a decent cash reserve to ride out the slow times, but he wasn't going to throw that away just to keep production happening. The more he produced, the more glut in the market.

"Sheesh, Gage, what is with you tonight? You just zoned out again." Gavin commented.

Something nudged his leg. Merle. He reached out and scratched the dog behind the ear. At least someone was trying to make him feel better. "I've been traveling for a month straight. I'm tired, okay? And if you hadn't noticed, the price of oil is at an all-time fucking low."

"Shit, man, sorry. I appreciate you coming down here," Grayson said. "I know how much you really don't like Sweet Ridge."

Holy hell, why did everyone think he hated Sweet Ridge? He'd simply made a life for himself in Houston. And sure, he and Dad had fallen out when he'd lost his scholarship and his potential career as an NFL player. But he had good memories of Sweet Ridge. If he'd been given the land like he thought he was, he'd have even started spending weekends down at the house before he started drilling. There was a lot of preparation to be done to set up a drill site.

"I don't hate Sweet Ridge. But if you don't start talking about something other than me, I will be leaving."

Grayson held up his hands in surrender. "Fine. I wanted to know if you had any idea what direction you want Guac Olé to go in, now that you and Gavin have a controlling interest between the two of you."

"We don't have controlling interest. We have half, and quite frankly I've got my own business to worry about. I can't really spend time worrying about what Guac Olé is doing," Gage said. "I trust you, Gray, to keep the company going the way Dad would've wanted it. I don't get why he didn't give you the company."

"Well, I ended up getting what I wanted," Gavin replied. "In a most unexpected way. But you know what I found out?"

"What?" Gage and Grayson said in unison.

"That at the end of the day what I thought I coveted wasn't what I really wanted at all. Maybe the old man knew what he was doing after all."

Gage snorted. "Please, you're in love. Everything looks rosy at the moment. I could do with that piece of land right now. Once the price of oil picks up, I could jump right in and employ back some of those people I've had to lay off over the last month."

Before his brothers could say anything more, Gage's phone beeped with an incoming e-mail. He would've ignored it, but Charlotte's name popped up with the subject heading "Inherited Land." He unlocked his phone and opened the email.

Hi Gage,

I've been doing some thinking about our current dilemma with regards to the land I inherited from your father. I've made the decision that, with the fact my time here in Texas is running out, I don't want to be stuck with a piece of land while I'm living on the other side of the world. I plan to contact Jack's lawyer in the morning and set in motion the necessary steps to sell you the land. I don't know how much it's valued at, but I'm sure the lawyer can work out a fair price that will make us both happy.

Once I know something, I will be in touch.

Best regards,

Charlotte

He had to read the e-mail twice. Was she kidding him? He hoped not.

"I take it from the smile on your face that price of oil has doubled today?" Grayson asked.

Gage looked up. "I wish, but it's something even better. Charlotte Wilkinson said she'd sell me the land. Looks like I don't need to fall in love to get everything I want."

Chapter 4

"I'm really sorry, Ms. Wilkinson, but Mr. Cooper's will was very explicit. You cannot sell the land for twelve months."

This wasn't the news she wanted to hear. "Is that even legal to put a stipulation like that in a will? I mean, Jack knew I wasn't staying in Texas for much longer. I still don't get why he did this."

"I can assure you, Ms. Wilkinson, everything within Jack Cooper's will is legal."

Charlotte cringed when she heard the indignation in the lawyer's voice. Way to go. Get the one person who could help you offside with a single sentence.

"Look, Mr. Rodgers, I didn't mean to imply you would do anything unethical. It's just that I'm still in shock about receiving this bequest at all. As I said to you after you initially informed me of my inheritance, I'd only met Jack a few times. It really doesn't make sense why he would leave me something so tangible and valuable. Especially when it seems his son Gage was expecting to receive the land."

"I understand how much of a shock this was for you, but I've known Jack Cooper for a very long time. He knew what he was doing with his will. His sons will soon come to see that. Now, I have a meeting I need to get to. Call if you need anything further, but I will repeat: You can't sell the land."

"Like I need reminding," she muttered as the lawyer disconnected the call.

Charlotte threw her phone down on her desk. What she was going to do next? Perhaps she should take a trip out to Sweet Ridge and see just what she'd inherited. For all she knew, it could just be a small strip of land that held no consequence at all. Although it seemed unlikely Gage would be this possessive if it were only a meaningless piece of dirt.

He'd been passionate about wanting the land when he'd been in her office. Even his e-mail response of purchasing it at any price she asked indicated it could be worth a pretty penny.

Maybe she should get the land valued.

A knock on the door sounded and she looked up to see her manager hovering in the doorway.

"Hey, Allen, what's up?"

"Have you got a minute? There's some news I need to discuss with you."

"Certainly."

She hoped it was good news after the disappointing tidbit she'd received from the lawyer. Maybe he was going to tell her they were extending her contract. When she'd first arrived there had been talk about a possible extension, but as the end of her contract drew closer and closer, the prospect of returning to Australia seemed the more likely outcome.

She attempted to contain her thoughts as she followed Allen down the hall. She wanted to stay longer. She had so much more to give to the firm. But it could be something completely different that he wanted to talk about. Though the company was small, it seemed very busy. They could have another project for her to review.

"Take a seat, Charlotte," Allen directed as he took his own place at the head of the boardroom.

Charlotte smiled at the other occupants of the room. This had to be serious if the other two partners were also in the room.

Allen cleared his throat. "Charlotte, we've been very happy with the service you've provided the company over the last four months. As you know, we hired you on a six-month contract with the possibility of an extension. Your visa is a temporary work visa. We deliberately did this for a couple of reasons. One of them was, while you came highly recommended to us, we hadn't worked with you before and we didn't want to commit to a long-term contract if you didn't fit in with our firm. We knew after a week that wouldn't be an issue."

"Thank you, Allen. I really enjoy working here. It's been a great challenge," she interjected.

"We're glad you feel that way. Another reason for the temporary visa was because of our long-term plans. If we felt you were suitable and it became obvious to us that you enjoyed working and living in the United States, we would look at commencing a green card process if you were interested."

The excitement bubble took on a life of its own. She loved working in the States. She'd grown up an ex-pat kid, so she'd lived in Australia off and on during her life. Only it never felt like her real home. Maybe because she'd traveled around so much she had no idea what home really meant. One of the longest periods she had stayed in Australia had been while she completed her final two years of high school and the years it took to get her environmental science degree. But once she started working, she'd started to feel restless, like she needed something more, something bigger in her life than living and working in Sydney. She'd identified the feeling as itchy feet, so when the opportunity to work for Gold Star Eco had come up, she'd jumped at it.

"I'm very interested in this opportunity, Allen. I've been hoping you would extend my contract, as I feel I have so much more to give."

"Excellent. We will look into what we have to do and the cost involved with this process. We've never done anything like this before. In fact, you are our first international employee, so it's all unchartered waters for us, as well."

"You won't be disappointed with your decision. I'll make sure of it."

•••

Charlotte pulled into the Sweet Ridge Inn's car park. It had taken her longer than she'd anticipated to head down to Sweet Ridge.

It seemed everyone wanted to head out of town this particular weekend and the roads had been chaotic. If there was one thing she disliked about living in Houston, it was the traffic. People were crazy on the roads. Their love affair for talking or texting as they drove astounded her.

She got out of the car, grabbed her overnight bag, and headed to reception. Within minutes she was getting into an elevator and making her way to her room. Once she'd dumped her bag, she was going to head to Betty Lou's Diner and grab a bite to eat. Maybe bring back some donuts for breakfast.

It felt good to be back in Sweet Ridge. The laid-back atmosphere reminded her of the small town where she and her family had vacationed at one time when they'd returned to Australia for a break between her father's assignments.

After a quick visit to the bathroom and a change of clothes, she headed out the door again. It would only take her a few minutes to walk to the diner. Outside, she took a couple of deep breaths. It was nice to breathe in fresh air, not the air tainted by car exhaust she sometimes breathed in in Houston.

The early evening sun softened the outline of the buildings, giving them a romantic feel. She was excited about tomorrow, when she'd take a drive to see the land.

Charlotte reached the cute-looking diner and pulled open the door. Immediately her senses came alive as the aroma of donuts and fried foods greeted her. The diner had an old-fashioned feel to it, with its counter where you could sit and peer through to the kitchen to see the line cooks making up the orders. The booths had turquoise leather seats and Formica countertops. It was like a step back in time to when the town's diner was the place to be seen.

"Charlotte, honey, is that you?"

Charlotte turned and the diner's namesake, Betty Lou, enveloped her in a big hug as a greeting. Even Betty Lou looked like a throwback from the 1950s with her beehive hairstyle and funky red glasses.

She returned the hug, surprised Betty Lou remembered her from her previous visits. "It's good to see you. And you've got a good memory."

Betty Lou laughed. "It's hard to forget a girl with hair as lovely as you have, not to mention your pretty accent. But it's been a while." She sobered a little. "I'm sorry, I have some news about Jack."

Charlotte squeezed the diner owner's hand. "I know he's passed away."

While part of her wanted to let Betty Lou know about her inheritance, she kept that bit of information to herself. She was sure it would all come out in good time.

Betty Lou wiped her eyes. "It was a sad day when Jack Cooper left this earth. His presence will be felt for years to come, though. He did an awful lot of good for this town. Now, let me show you to a table. How long are you in town for? If you knew about Jack's death, what brings you back?"

Charlotte's mind whirled with the questions fired at her, but she answered them as Betty Lou showed to her a corner booth with a window looking at out the main street. "I like Sweet Ridge and realized it's been a while since I've been here. I thought a weekend away might be nice. I also want to explore the place a little more."

"That's good, sweetie. Here's a menu. Today's donut special is Lemon Sizzle. It's sour with a bite."

While Charlotte appreciated Betty Lou's ingenuity in coming up with different flavors, when it came to donuts, she liked hers plain and coated with sprinkled sugar.

"Thanks. I think I'll make my donut decision after I've had some of your fabulous fried chicken and mashed potatoes. Can I also have a glass of Coke, please?"

"Coming right up. Anything el—" The bell above the diner door tinkled, signaling the arrival of another patron and distracting Betty Lou. "Macy! Over here, sweetie. I want you to meet someone."

A girl a few years older than her, dressed in a cute slip dress and wearing cowboy boots and a cowboy hat, approached the table.

Betty Lou greeted her with the same sort of hug she'd given Charlotte. "Macy, this is Charlotte, from Australia. Charlotte, this is Macy. She's a famous country-and-western music star."

"Hi, Macy, it's nice to meet you."

"Hey, Charlotte, it's good to meet you, too. Australia, huh? That's one place I'd love to visit one day. Y'alls accent is so cool. Do you mind if I join you?"

"No, please do. And thank you. Everyone always comments on my accent. I don't see what's so special about it."

Macy sat down and Charlotte tried to think if she'd heard any of Macy's music. She wasn't a big country-and-western listener, although she'd come across the odd station or fifty on her satellite radio.

"It's just so pretty. And sounds so proper." Macy turned to Betty Lou. "Can I have an iced tea and your chicken fried steak special?"

"Sure, Macy. You not eating with Gavin?"

"Not tonight. He's eating with his brothers, but I'm meeting him at the Silver Spurs later on."

"You should take Charlotte, introduce her to Gage and Grayson," Betty Lou said with a wink before walking away. "Those boys could do with someone pretty in their lives."

Surely there couldn't be two Gages living in Sweet Ridge. And surely, fate wouldn't be so cruel as to throw Gage in her path again when she was visiting town to see the very land he wanted.

"Please tell me she's not talking about Gage Cooper." She directed her question to Macy, who was humming and drumming her fingers on the table.

"Yep, why? Do you know Gage?"

For all Charlotte knew, Macy could be one of his ex-lovers or something. A high-profile star seemed the sort of girl Gage would chase after.

"Umm, yes, I do. You could say our paths have crossed one or two times."

Macy leaned forward, a gleam in her eye. "Ohhh, now you've got me intrigued. Don't tell me the two of you dated."

Charlotte laughed out loud. "No, definitely not. Our interactions have purely been professional."

Macy sat back. "Well, now, that's disappointing. I thought you'd have something I could use to dangle over his head. Or at least tell Gavin about so he and Grayson could torment him with it."

Another waitress arrived with a tray loaded up with their food and drinks. Once she placed their meals in front of them, Charlotte asked Macy the question burning in the front of her mind.

"How well do you know Gage?"

"We all went to the same high school—me, Gavin, Grayson, and Gage—although I was just starting my senior year when he was a freshman. I did expect Gage to be a big- time football player taking my team, the Dallas Cowboys, to the Super Bowl. He was the star player on the high school team. Everyone was talking about what a great future he was going to have."

Charlotte filed away that piece of information. Never would she have thought Gage would've been a football player. He seemed way more at home in an office than on an expanse of green grass. "I don't know that much about American football."

"We breathe football here in Texas. I'm dating Gage's older brother now, and when I asked why Gage is in oil and not the NFL, Gavin clammed up. I'm guessing there's a story there, but I'm more interested in my man than his brother."

A soft smile broke out over Macy's face. She could tell that Macy cared a lot for Gage's brother, but Charlotte was more intrigued by the story of why Gage hadn't followed through on his potential to be a superstar football player.

"Actually, dating is pretty tame to describe what is going on between us. Gavin is the love of my life. I inherited a beautiful house, and I'm so happy I could burst."

Bells started ringing in Charlotte's head, and all thoughts of delving further into Gage's non-football career disappeared. Not the "*Danger, Will Robinson!*" type bells. More of the "*something is familiar here*" type.

"You inherited a house? I'm sorry for your loss. Was it a close family member who died?"

To her astonishment, Macy laughed. Who laughed over someone's death? Unless they didn't like that person and were glad they'd passed on. Even though Charlotte hadn't known Jack a long time, she had felt extremely sad when she'd heard the news.

Macy touched her arm, obviously seeing her surprise. "Jack Cooper was a wily old bastard and I loved him, even though I hadn't seen much of him since I left high school. Gavin and I used to compete with each other academically in high school. Jack saw it, and sometimes he would encourage me to challenge Gavin because he knew it would make his son work harder. He had a backward method, and maybe he saw something we didn't see as kids. Anyway, it's because of the house that Gavin and I reconnected again. Sorry if I shocked you with my laughter—it's because I know Jack is looking down on us with a big smile on his face."

Jack had left Macy a house? And he'd left her a piece of land. Should she mention that to Macy or not? If she did, would Macy think the same as Gage, that she'd tricked Jack into making her a beneficiary of his will?

She'd keep her inheritance to herself for a little while longer.

They ate their meal, making small talk about general things. Macy seemed so down-to-earth for a country star, and the people of Sweet Ridge let her eat in peace. Maybe because she grew up in town they weren't as star struck by her.

"So, are you a big country-and-western music fan, Charlotte?"

"Ahh, not really. I don't listen to it much. Sorry."

Macy chuckled. "It's okay. You either love country music or you don't. I won't hold it against you."

"Thanks." Charlotte pushed her plate forward. "I swear if I lived here, I would put on so much weight. Betty Lou's fried chicken is the best."

"Tell me about it. I've had to make sure I keep up with my exercising, otherwise I'd be stacking on the pounds, too. I'm a judge on *America's Next Country Star*, and we've just started filming again. The cameras add pounds." She laughed as she said it. "Have you had Betty Lou's donuts? I swear I tried every donut shop in Nashville to find something that tasted half as good as Betty Lou's with no luck."

"Yep, I have and I'm addicted to them, too. I'm thinking of getting some to take back to the hotel with me so I can have them for breakfast."

"Well, make sure you get one of the orange-flavored ones. They are to die for."

Not wanting to offend Macy, she nodded. "I'll have to do that."

Charlotte slid out of the booth. "It's been great meeting you, Macy. Maybe I'll see you again this weekend in my travels."

"Oh no, girl, you can't leave yet. Betty Lou would take me to task if I let you go back to a lonely hotel room. You're coming with me to the Silver Spurs."

The last place Charlotte wanted to be was anywhere near Gage Cooper. Although, would he act differently in a relaxed, non-work environment? Would he let his animosity toward her show, or would he be pleasant in front of his brothers?

As much as she was tempted to throw Gage off-balance by turning up at the local watering hole, she thought better of it. She had to set up a meeting with him or at least call him to let him know that selling the land wasn't a possibility now.

"Thanks for the invite, but I don't want to intrude."

"Oh, girlfriend, trust me, you won't be intruding. Besides, I won't take no for an answer. So let's get your donuts, drop them off at your hotel, and then go to the bar."

Did she really want to spend the night alone in her hotel room? And who said she had to stay and hang around with Macy and the Cooper boys all night? She might find herself a cute cowboy to hang out with. Maybe she wouldn't need the work-sponsored green card after all. She could fall in love with a Texan and get married instead.

Charlotte laughed out loud at the absurd thought.

"What's so funny?"

"Nothing, just letting myself think pie-in-the-sky thoughts. But okay, I would like to see the Silver Spurs and spend some time with you. Thanks, Macy."

"You're welcome. It's going to be fun. Trust me." A wicked gleam entered Macy's eye.

What had she just agreed to?

Chapter 5

Gage eyed the multicolored balls scattered across the pool table. Grayson snickered in his ear.

"Snookered you real good, didn't I?"

"Whatever. Now move, so I can whip your ass."

"Whatever you say, little brother. Whatever you say. But this game is mine. Like always."

Gage laughed at his brother's antics. He had to admit, he was glad he'd made the time to come to Sweet Ridge. He'd spent the day walking the perimeter of the land he would soon own. He planned to head out there again tomorrow to take photos to send to his survey people.

"Geez, Gage, watching you decide what to do is like watching paint dry. I'm going to be turning gray if you take too much longer to sink a ball. Macy's not gonna love me with gray hair."

"Aww, baby, I'll still love you when you're old and wrinkly."

Gage looked up and almost dropped his cue when he spied who was standing behind Macy.

What the hell was Charlotte Wilkinson doing in Sweet Ridge? And why the hell was she with Macy, of all people?

Her chin rose a notch, like she knew what he was thinking. She certainly didn't look shocked to see him.

Gavin finally released Macy, and Miss TV Personality walked over, dragging Charlotte with her.

"Gage, darlin'. Good to see you again." He accepted the kiss Macy placed on his cheek.

"You, too, Macy. Although I have to wonder what's happened to that smart brain of yours, hooking up with a doofus like Gavin."

Macy laughed and shrugged. "What can I say? I love him."

"Well, there's no accounting for taste," Gage said drily and smiled when Macy hit him on the shoulder.

"Babe, aren't you going to introduce us to your friend?" Gavin came to stand by his girl.

"Oh, yes. This here is Charlotte Wilkinson. I had dinner with her at the diner after Betty Lou introduced us. Actually, she insisted that I meet Charlotte. I'm glad she did. Although Gage already knows Charlotte, don't you?"

"Yes, I do. It's good to see you again, Charlotte. What brings you to Sweet Ridge?"

"Gage." She inclined her head like she was the queen of England and he was a lowly servant.

He had a feeling he knew exactly why she was here.

"This is Charlotte Wilkinson?" Grayson whistled long and low. "Bro, you've been holding out on us. I wonder why."

Gage's temper simmered below the surface.

"Hello, Charlotte Wilkinson," Grayson drawled. "I'm Grayson, the best Cooper brother of the lot."

Charlotte smiled. "Hello, Grayson. The best brother, huh? Guess we'll see if that's true."

"Ignore him, Charlotte." Gage sent him a *back off* look, and Grayson laughed.

"Hang on a minute," Gavin burst out. "Charlotte Wilkinson. You inherited Gage's piece of land from Dad, didn't you? Why are you here?"

"Leave it, Gavin. It doesn't matter." His tone was harsh, letting both his brothers know he would take them to task if they continued to be jerks toward Charlotte. It surprised the hell out of him that he lifted a finger to help her. Wasn't she supposed to be his enemy?

"Thanks, Gage, but I don't need your help." Charlotte looked first at Gavin and then Grayson. "Yes, I did inherit land from your dad. I liked Jack, and I wasn't expecting the inheritance. And that's all I'm going to say on the issue. What I do with that land is none of your concern."

Fine, she didn't need his help. And seeing the stunned looks on Gavin and Grayson's faces, they hadn't expected her to stand up to them.

"Ha, you boys just got burned." Macy laughed loudly. "How can you be angry when you get told off in that cool accent?"

"Easily," Grayson muttered.

Gage had enough. Another minute of this shit and his bad mood would start a new family rift.

He handed his cue to Macy, who automatically took it. "See if you can whip Gray's butt. I'm going to get Charlotte a drink."

Not waiting to see what his brothers did, Gage cupped Charlotte by the elbow and led her through the tables until they reached the bar. The noise level here was higher than in the corner where the pool tables were located.

He leaned down and spoke into her ear. "What can I get you to drink?"

Charlotte repeated his action. "Classic mojito, please."

Her lips brushed his ear and his body stirred to life. What the fuck? He managed to conceal the unexpected shiver from her. How could he want to take her to the corner and have her whisper to him some more when she had been nothing but a pain in the ass to him? He couldn't deny what Macy had said about her accent being cool. He'd thought the accent was all prissy on the phone, but in person, it was sexy as hell.

Dragging his thoughts out of the gutter, he gave their order to the bartender and turned so his back rested against the wooden bar.

"So, why are you here, Charlotte?" he spoke loudly enough to be heard over the background noise.

"Here as in the bar, or here as in Sweet Ridge?"

"Both."

"Well, you know why I'm here at the bar—Macy invited me. And as for being in Sweet Ridge, I figured it was time I saw the piece of land I inherited."

He wanted to ask her whether she'd spoken to the lawyer about selling the land to him, but the middle of a bar on a Friday night was hardly the place to do it. Still, he couldn't wait to sign the papers granting him ownership. He would ensure he paid her a fair price. Fuck it, what did it matter if he asked her now? He opened his mouth to speak.

Charlotte placed a finger on his mouth, and his whole body zeroed in on her touch. "Don't do it."

"Do what?"

"I see the look in your face, Gage. I know you want to ask, but can we please not do this tonight? I just want to enjoy my drink and then go back to the hotel. I don't want to get into any discussions about land or inheritances."

He saw the tiredness in Charlotte's eyes. He could relate to the look. He'd had a hell of a week, and not fifteen minutes ago he'd been enjoying his brothers' company. Why not continue to unwind on a Friday night and leave inheritance issues alone?

"Fair enough. Do you want to meet for breakfast or lunch tomorrow?"

"Lunch sounds good. Do you want to meet at Betty Lou's Diner?"

Not even a raised eyebrow in surprise at his suggestion. Nothing seemed to rattle Charlotte Wilkinson.

"Not unless you want the whole town to know your business. Betty Lou isn't happy unless she's finding out what everyone is up to. I don't go to the diner. How about we meet here instead? It's not as busy as this on a Saturday afternoon."

"That works, say twelve thirty?"

The bartender arrived with their drinks. Gage handed him some money and picked up their drinks. "Yep. Now, do you want to go back to my lovely brothers and Macy, or do you want to see if we can find a table?"

"If it's okay with you, I'd rather head back to where your brothers are. I think they know where I stand now and won't give me too much hassle."

"Okay." He began to weave through the crowd again. He made sure Charlotte was by his side. "I think they've learned their lesson. Unless, of course, they do decide to torment you like older brothers do just so they can hear you tell them off in your *cool* accent."

Charlotte shook her head. "Seriously, I have no idea why my accent fascinates everyone so much."

He could tell her that he found her accent sexy and wished she'd whisper to him all night. He knew it wouldn't be appreciated if he voiced his thoughts. Even he was having issues with why he was becoming fascinated with her when two days ago he was ripping her character to shreds. With the way she handled his brothers, he had no doubt she'd captivated Dad with her bright personality and intelligence, and Jack Cooper would've been smitten by her accent, too. "That's because it's so different and proper and as Macy said, 'cool.'"

"You're all crazy, and really you don't have to worry about me when it comes to your brothers. I've got three older ones. I can hold my own."

"I'll just bet you can," he said below his breath.

"Hey, where are our drinks?" Grayson complained when Gage and Charlotte arrived back at the pool table. He placed their drinks on the high table.

"Yeah, why isn't the oil baron shouting a round of drinks for us?" Gavin piped in. "Oh, and before I forget, I need you at the clinic tomorrow morning. I've got something for you that I know you're going to love."

"I'll be there when you open. With regards to your drinks, they're at the bar, where you can go and order them yourselves.

Besides, I'm not going to be seen ordering Gray's girlie gin and tonic. I've got a reputation to maintain."

Gavin snorted. "Good one, Gage."

He should make more of an effort to spend time with them. He'd cut himself off because he'd fucked up his life and couldn't stand to see the disappointment in their eyes. It was bad enough to see it in Dad's eye. All of the Coopers had wanted him to get drafted to one of the Texas teams; Gavin and Dad didn't care if it was the Texans or the Cowboys, but Gray was Cowboys all the way. He'd often joked with them about being drafted by the Patriots or Seahawks, but at the end of the day they wanted him close to them.

And then when his dream had blown up amidst underage drinking, breaking athletic curfew, and fraternity pranks, he'd gone and left them anyway. Cut himself off totally.

"Hey, where did you go?" A soft hand touching his arm pulled him from his dark thoughts.

"Down the lonely path called memory lane."

"Didn't look like it was a pleasant journey."

It was amazing how, when he focused solely on Charlotte, all the outside noise from the bar disappeared and they were in a vacuum of silence.

"It is what it is, and I have to live with the choices I made. But this isn't why we're here." He allowed the noise back in to consume his dark thoughts. Bar noise was much better than the noise of his own voice telling him what a fuckup he was.

"I wonder where Macy is," Charlotte said.

Thank God she wasn't going to press him for an explanation of his thoughts.

"She's getting ready to sing a couple of songs. Steve came over and asked if she'd sing," Gavin said. "I can't wait."

"Bro, you're telling us she doesn't sing at home for you? Doesn't she sing sweet lullabies to help you sleep at night?" teased Gage.

"Ha ha ha, very funny. Yes, she does sing. I love her voice. I never get sick of hearing it."

Gage made a gagging sound. "Oh, please, keep your lovesickness to yourself."

"I think it's sweet," Charlotte commented.

Gage opened his mouth to fire a smart-ass comment, but stopped himself when he saw her quirked eyebrow. She fully expected him to say something snarky.

Instead he brought his bottle of beer to his lips to take a drink.

Conversation became impossible as the bar crowd started chanting Macy's name, with Gavin leading the charge. Gage sat back and watched his oldest brother. He'd never seen Gavin like this. So open and happy and clearly in love. Would he ever give himself totally to a woman like Gavin had?

"I love you, baby," Macy said into the microphone and waved to their corner before she started belting out one of her number-one hits.

When you had someone as totally in love with you as Macy was with Gavin, he supposed it would be easy to let your guard down and embrace what they had to offer.

He chanced a look at Charlotte to see what she thought of the exchange. She was cheering and laughing, as well. She moved her chair so she had a better view of the stage. She looked beautiful. Her red hair glittered beneath the low barroom light, reminding him of the glow from a fire. Her foot tapped along with the music, her attention totally on Macy as she played to the crowd.

A few songs later Macy segued into a ballad. A space had opened up and couples started to fill it, swaying to the haunting tune about regrets and wishes to change the past. To start over and beg for forgiveness. He could totally relate.

Someone jabbed him in the ribs. That someone was Grayson.

"Ask Charlotte to dance," he encouraged.

"I don't dance," Gage responded.

"You danced every time you avoided those defensive linemen out on the football field. Swaying to some music won't be that difficult."

Gage had to admit, it was a valid excuse to get Charlotte in his arms.

"If you don't ask her, I will," Grayson taunted.

"Shove it, Gray." He pushed his chair back, the wooden legs scraping along the floor.

He walked around the table to where Charlotte sat. He squatted down so she could hear him. "Would you like to dance?"

Her head whipped around and her hair flew around his face. He caught the sweet scent of coconuts, which he guessed came from her shampoo. "What did you say?"

"I asked if you'd like to dance."

"Yes, I'd like that."

Gage stood and held out his hand. She took it and he made his way toward the group of people dancing. Macy caught his eye and winked, giving him a thumbs-up. He rolled his eyes. He was having one dance, then it was time he left. He didn't need to hang around to give his brothers and Macy any matchmaking ideas.

He turned Charlotte and looped his arms around her waist. She placed her hands on his shoulders. The distance between their two bodies was big enough for another person to stand between them as they moved stiltedly side by side. To an onlooker they probably looked like two reluctant teenagers who'd been dared to dance together at their first school dance. It was ridiculous, and he was a lot smoother than this.

Flexing his shoulders, he made himself relax. He pulled Charlotte close so their bodies touched chest to chest, thigh to thigh. Her arms made their way around his neck and she rested her head against his shoulder.

Now they swayed naturally, their bodies moving in time with the beat of Macy's song. He closed his eyes and let himself get carried away on the music. He breathed in the scent of coconuts again and smiled. He could get used to this. And that was something he couldn't let happen.

Chapter 6

A descending musical tone played over and over in Charlotte's mind. She wanted it to go away. She wanted to go back to her dream. She groaned. She'd forgotten to turn off her cell phone alarm. Of all the weekends to forget, it had to be this one.

Pulling herself up on her elbow, she reached for her phone and disengaged the alarm. She flopped back onto the pillow and let her mind drift back to the dream she'd been jolted out of. She'd been dancing in Gage's arms again. Macy was singing a beautiful song just for them. The part she wanted to block out was the memory of where they were and what she was wearing. Unfortunately, her mind wouldn't let her have dream amnesia, and the picture of her in a wedding dress and Gage looking spectacular in tuxedo wouldn't fade away.

Why on earth was she having dreams about marrying Gage? Three days ago he was an annoying oilman who fought her every suggestion. Just because they'd been able to spend a pleasant evening together didn't mean they were destined to be married. For all she knew, if she couldn't get a green card or her contract extended, she'd be back on a plane to Sydney in two months.

That thought didn't bear thinking about. She had to believe she would be able to stay in Texas.

Now that the seed of possibly staying had been planted, it was going to take a lot for it not to take root. She should start thinking about where she would live. It would be so good if Jack's land had a house on it. If it was habitable, then she'd turn it into a weekend place. She'd put up with the horrid traffic on a Friday afternoon if she knew she had a retreat down here in Sweet Ridge. It would be the perfect way to end a busy workweek. Not to mention she'd be able to see Macy regularly. The other woman had given Charlotte her contact details when she left the bar the previous evening.

The appeal of having a weekend place had nothing to do with the possibility of seeing Gage on the odd occasion. It was more than likely she would see him in a business environment rather than a casual run-in at the Silver Spurs. Now that she couldn't sell the land and with the chance she would be staying permanently, it didn't seem too wrong to make plans to keep the property and not sell it to Gage. Even though he would probably be upset at this change in plans, the land was hers to do with what she wanted. Jack had left it to her, not Gage.

Thinking of Gage reminded her they had a lunch date. If she wanted to see the property before she met up with him, then it was just as well she'd awakened early.

• • •

Two hours later Charlotte drove down a tree-lined driveway of what was the first piece of real estate she'd ever owned. She had no idea what was up ahead, but she couldn't wait.

A little farther up, the trees gave way to an expanse of green. "Oh my." The words escaped out of her.

Perched on a small rise was a quaint two-story white house with black-shuttered windows. Excitement coursed through her veins. Now that she'd seen the property, selling to Gage was even further from her mind. How could she part with something so adorable? There had to be a reason why Jack had left the land to her. Did it mean something?

So many questions she'd never know the answer to. She couldn't get ahead of herself. There was no point, not if her future wasn't in Texas.

Parking the car, she got out and walked briskly to the front door. The closer she got she was able to tell the house looked to be in good condition. It could probably do with a coat of paint. But it didn't look like it was about to collapse around her ears. The wooden porch creaked slightly when she stepped on it. She could picture giving the old timber a breath of life with a light sanding and some new stain. The possibilities were endless.

What about Gage? What about your offer of selling the place to him? You're not one to go back on your word.

No matter how much she tried to ignore it, the little annoying voice in her head demanded to be heard. It didn't matter what the voice said. She couldn't sell the property for a year. By then Gage might have lost interest and moved on to something else in his life.

She reached the front door and stopped.

Shit, the lawyer had told her to contact him if she planned to visit Sweet Ridge. When she'd called about selling the land she hadn't thought to ask him about the property. If she had, she would've found out there was a house and she could've arranged to get a key so she could look around.

Maybe there was a spare lying hidden beneath a faux rock. Or above the door frame. Or underneath a welcome mat.

Well, there was no welcome mat, so she ran her hand along the top of the door frame very carefully. The last thing she wanted or needed was to get a splinter. Disappointment filled her when she didn't come across a spare key. Walking back down the stairs, she inspected the rocks in the overgrown garden. Did one of them look like it didn't belong?

Nope, they all looked real. A little dejected and mad at herself for not thinking this plan through thoroughly, she headed around the back of the house. Repeating her action of feeling around the back door frame, she met with success.

A key.

Blowing the dust off it, she inserted it into the back door lock. It opened easily. She expected to be greeted by a dust cloud from years of neglect. That didn't happen. What greeted her was a dust-free mudroom. If she didn't know better, she'd say someone had cleaned the house the day before.

Buoyed by her find, she walked in and started to investigate. The mudroom led to a large airy kitchen. The countertops were laminate but seemed to be in good condition. Same with the kitchen cabinets. At some stage the kitchen would need to be updated, but for the time being it would provide the most basic of amenities.

She made her way through the kitchen to the living room when she heard what sounded like another car pulling into the driveway.

A sense of unease filled her. She stood in a house in the middle of nowhere. No one from town knew she'd come out here. No one apart from the Cooper family knew she had come to town. She had nothing to defend herself with, unless there happened to be a knife in the kitchen drawer.

Charlotte sidled up to the window. Pushing aside the curtain, she watched a sleek-looking sports car pull up beside her mundane sedan.

She didn't know much about serial killers, but she was pretty sure they didn't drive late model sports cars.

A tall figure stepped out.

Gage.

What the hell was he doing here? And what did he have on the end of what looked like a leash—a cat or the smallest dog in history? Gage didn't strike her as a small dog kind of guy. A German shepherd or a Rottweiler, yes. A frou-frou dog? No way.

She marched over to the front door. Maybe the key in her hand was dual function and unlocked the back and front doors. She'd never know until she tried.

Charlotte inserted the key in the door and turned. The satisfying sound of the lock unbolting echoed around the room.

She opened the door and walked out onto the porch.

"I'm afraid I've got nothing for unexpected visitors."

If she thought she'd surprised him last night at the bar, it was nothing like the incredulous look on his face at hearing her voice.

"Charlotte? What are you doing here?"

"Well, I could say the same to you, seeing as how you're trespassing on what is essentially my property."

A flash of black darted out from behind Gage, pulling his arm and jerking him off his feet.

"God dammit, Oil Slick, come back here."

She laughed as he gave the lead a slight yank and the animal immediately halted in its attempt to escape or chase something. She wasn't quite sure what the animal was doing.

She traipsed down the steps and ambled over to Gage. She could finally make out it wasn't a dog at the end of the leash but a cute, black kitten. How could it be a cat, though. Cats didn't like leashes.

"Is that a cat?"

"No, what it is, is Gavin's idea of a sick joke. He and Macy talked me into taking the cat Macy hit with her car."

As she got closer she could see a scar on the back of its leg where the fur had yet to grow over. The cat, with its inquisitive nature, pranced over to where she stood and immediately began sniffing her outstretched hand like a dog.

She smiled up at Gage. "I suspect your cat thinks it's a dog. I've never seen a cat so happy to be attached to a leash."

Gage bent down and picked up the furry creature. Straight away, it head-butted Gage for a pat. "Tell me about it. But I guess hanging out with Gavin's dog, Merle, she picked up some of the dog's habits and mannerisms. All the way down here in the car, she sat quietly on the passenger seat. I had to check a couple of times to make sure she was still breathing."

"I thought cats hated cars."

"Yeah, and you'd think after being hit by one, Oil Slick here would dislike them."

"Oil Slick? What sort of name is that for a cat?"

"It's better than the name they were calling her."

"What was that?"

"Lady Marceline."

"Well, it's prettier than the name you've given her."

"She's my cat now, I get to name her what I want. Besides"—Gage shrugged—"I thought Oil Slick fit her well. I'm in the oil industry. She's black and she was almost a slick on the road."

Charlotte snorted, she couldn't help it. "What an awful analogy."

"Maybe, but she likes it." He tickled the cat around her ears. "Don't you, Oil Slick?"

The cat purred loudly in response. God, who knew Gage holding a kitten could be so incredibly sexy? What was it about guys holding small puppies and kittens that sent girls into a puddle of hormones? Even if the guys holding them were jerks.

She watched as he kept scratching Oil Slick behind her ears. He might have taken the cat under sufferance, but it seemed he was smitten by the little creature as much as Oil Slick was smitten with Gage. And why wouldn't Oil Slick be happy? Being held in Gage's arms last night had felt wonderful. Something Charlotte could easily get used to.

She gave herself a mental shake. "Why are you here?"

He shifted uncomfortably and she went on high alert. What was he up to? Well, whatever it was, he was about to get a rude shock when she told him she couldn't sell to him. And now that she'd seen the property, she didn't want to sell it. She knew that wasn't going to go down very well with him.

He made a production of putting the cat back on the ground.

"You know how I mentioned previously I have older brothers," she said casually.

Gage looked up. "Yeah."

"Well, I've observed them lie to my parents. Each one has a different tell. I know you're up to something. There's no point trying to lie your way out of it. Just come out and tell me what you're doing here."

He huffed out a breath. "Fine. I came here to walk the perimeter again."

"Again? That would suggest you've been here before. Are we talking years ago, or are we talking days ago?"

She wouldn't have obtained the high levels in her career if she hadn't been astute and listened carefully to what people around her said. As a woman in a male-oriented industry, she'd learned some men thought she was more eye candy than anything of intellectual use. She'd proven on more than one occasion she wasn't one to be messed with. And with their past dealings, she would've thought Gage would've realized that.

"I was here yesterday. I mean, soon it's going to be my land, so I figured I'd get a head start and see what I needed to do to the property. House looks like it's in pretty good shape, doesn't it?"

"Yes, it does. But with regards to the sale of the land…"

Gage's back stiffened and his head whipped around from his observation of the roof to look at her. All signs indicated he was on high alert, like she'd been a few minutes ago.

"What about the sale?" he asked warily.

She knew Gage's demeanor was about to change. She spied the cat; maybe she should suggest he pick it up.

"I spoke to Mr. Rodgers, your father's lawyer. The one who drew up the will."

"I know who Rodney Rodgers is. He's been around the family for years."

"Well, it seems your father put a stipulation into the will." She paused.

"Oh, for frig's sake, Charlotte, just spit it out. This isn't a soap opera. You don't have to stop for intense pauses and pathetic eyebrow raises to get across that something bad is about to happen. All we need is for dramatic music to start playing and the scene will be complete."

"I'm not trying to be melodramatic. But I know how much you wanted this land, and, well, I can't sell it for a year. Your dad put in a twelve-month no sale clause. I couldn't sell it to you even if I wanted to." She looked back over to the house. "And I don't think I want to now."

"What? You cannot be serious," he yelled while Oil Slick jumped and meowed in annoyance. She couldn't believe her eyes—that tiny cat had the power to make him bend down and scoop her up and murmur softly to her.

"I'm sorry, but I am serious. I don't think I want to sell after all."

Still holding the cat, he looked at her, his eyes cold with anger and disappointment. "Why would you hold land when Texas isn't even your home?"

"How do you know it's not my home?"

"Oh, come on, you're Australian. You're probably here on a work visa and work contract. All those things expire."

"So what if I'm Australian? It doesn't mean I have to go back and live there. I love it here. And my company wants to hire me permanently, so they're going to sponsor a green card application for me."

Yeah, she was bending the truth a little. Looking into the prospect of helping her obtain a green card was a bit different than actually going ahead with it. They'd cautioned her there could be unforeseen obstacles.

But she didn't want to think there could be issues. She was hoping that by the end of next week her application process would be started.

"I don't understand any of this," Gage muttered and put the cat back on the ground. "What the hell was the old man thinking?"

"I can't answer that. And I truly am sorry, Gage. I told you I liked Sweet Ridge when you came to my office. I'd forgotten how much I enjoyed coming here until last night when I pulled into town. Now that I've seen the place"—she waved a hand behind her encompassing the house—"I know Jack must have worked out that my true home was here in Texas, and so he gave me one."

Gage snorted. "Oh, that's just so *lovely*, isn't it? My father, the insightful one. Well, if he was so damn insightful, why did he leave me with twenty-five percent of a company I don't want to own and have no interest in, as well as a stupid key with some cryptic note? He promised me, dammit, he promised me this land."

"I'm sorry, Gage. I know it must be frustrating for you to think you were getting something only to have it snatched away."

"Save it. You know nothing. I don't think it's necessary to have lunch now," he retorted before he stormed toward his car, Oil Slick scampering behind him.

Her heart bled a little as she took in the house and the surrounding land. As much as she might dislike Gage, she didn't enjoy hurting him. Why did this land mean so much to Gage? Why was he fighting so hard to get it?

Why *did* Jack leave it to her?

Chapter 7

"Geez, cat, will you leave me alone?" Gage plucked Oil Slick off his desk again and put her on the ground. A second later she jumped back up and walked across his keyboard before sitting down beside his left hand. A mass of jumbled letters stood in the middle of an e-mail to a surveyor requesting a further assessment of a piece of land in Louisiana. He erased the letters Oil Slick had thought needed to be included in the e-mail, then quickly finished it. He hit send and closed down the program so the cat couldn't edit any more e-mails.

Even though the price of oil was at an all-time low, Gage wasn't going to sit on his laurels. Now he had a little time to investigate potential new sites so that when the price did indeed increase, and it would, he would be ready. Of course, he wouldn't have to make so many new plans if he'd inherited Dad's land. The likelihood of him owning it at all seemed impossible now. Especially after his run-in with Charlotte last weekend. He'd not even heard from her during the week with regard to more requests to make his rigs and operations safer on the environment.

He sighed and opened his desk drawer to pull out a fresh notepad and start brainstorming some ideas on possible new drilling sites instead of thinking about what might have been and Charlotte's e-mail silence.

Gage spied the note and key his father left him, sitting in the drawer. Instead of grabbing the pad, he picked up those items.

He didn't need to look at the note. The words were imprinted on his mind.

Son,

The key to everything is happiness.

Was he happy? He liked to think he was. Although he wasn't entirely happy at the moment. But prior to hearing that he couldn't buy the land off Charlotte, he'd been pretty damn happy with his lot in life.

And what was this *everything* his father was going on about? Did he mean achieving all his dreams and goals? Or was Dad talking about personal possessions? That seemed unlikely, considering Jack Cooper didn't hold stock in owning a lot of useless possessions. If it couldn't be used or worn, then it wasn't worth owning.

Oil Slick head-butted his hand. Without thinking, Gage scooped the little cat up and leaned back in his chair. It was clear the kitten was happy by the way she purred against his chest. Oil Slick had everything she needed: food, drink, the middle of his bed.

Making sure he didn't disturb the cat, he leaned forward and picked up the key. He'd looked through more images on the Internet the previous night to see if he could find something similar. He came up blank. It only reinforced his assumption the key belonged to a custom-made lock.

Only problem was, he couldn't recall ever seeing anything in his father's house that would fit the key. Although he hadn't been into the house for a few years, so Dad could've purchased the item the key belonged to and he hadn't known about it. Perhaps he should take another visit to Sweet Ridge and bug Gavin to let him check out the attic. Maybe the key belonged to something hidden up there.

"So, what do you think Dad means, Oil Slick?" he asked the kitten as he rubbed her ears. "If I find the object the key belongs to, do you think it means I'll find happiness?"

What he would probably need was admission into the psych ward at the local hospital if anyone found him talking to a cat.

His e-mail pinged, signaling incoming messages. He watched the screen as at least ten e-mails loaded up, but one in particular stood out—both by the person sending it and the subject line it contained. He tried not to get his hopes up just because the subject line read *Sweet Ridge Land* and the sender was Charlotte. Why was she e-mailing him on a Saturday morning? Maybe she was visiting Sweet Ridge again and had some questions about the land. It certainly wasn't because she'd had a change of heart and now wanted to sell it to him.

He clicked it open.

Hi, Gage,

I know we didn't part on the best of terms last weekend, but I was hoping, if you weren't too busy, that we might be able to meet for a coffee or maybe a walk in the park. I have something I need to discuss with you.

My cell is 555-325-2109.

Looking forward to hearing from you.

Regards,

Charlotte

Okay, this wasn't what he expected, but he certainly wasn't going to let his pride stop him from finding out what she wanted.

"Well, what do you know," he said to Oil Slick. "Our luck could be changing."

He gave the cat a quick pat on the head and then picked up his cell to dial Charlotte's number.

It rang for a while, and he expected it to go to voice mail when the call connected.

"Hello, Charlotte speaking."

His body perked to life hearing her breathless tone in his ear. "Hi, it's Gage. Did I catch you at a bad time?"

"Oh, hey, Gage, no, I was just on the treadmill when you called. Sorry it took me a while to pick up."

He wanted to ask her what she was wearing. He could picture her dressed in spandex, a crop top and those tight little shorts. Her long legs running rhythmically on the treadmill. Those same legs wrapped around his waist as he drove into her. He needed to go get laid if every time he spoke to Charlotte, he had fantasies about sleeping with her. God, she wasn't even really his type. He didn't go for redheads.

"Hello, are you there?"

He closed his eyes and took a couple of deep breaths. "Yeah, I'm here. Ahh, listen, I got your e-mail."

"Great, so does that mean you're free to meet?"

"Yeah, I am. Where exactly do you live?"

"I've got a place down in the Galleria District."

"Galleria District. Right."

"Is that a problem?"

Her accent made the question come out all prim and proper. "No, in fact, it's quite convenient. I live in the Galleria area, too."

"Oh, well, okay. That's handy."

"How about we meet at the Waterwall?"

"What time were you thinking?"

He glanced at the time on his laptop. "Why don't we make it midday? I'll pick up some food and drinks, and we can eat and talk about whatever it is you want to talk about."

"Sounds great. See you then."

"Bye."

The call disconnected. Anticipation fired through him. He hoped whatever Charlotte had to say, it would include the words "*I'll sell you my land.*"

• • •

Gage walked over to where the water thundered over the high granite walls. The Waterwall was a unique tourist attraction in

Houston, and on a Saturday afternoon there were a lot of people taking photos and filling the park area.

He had no idea where Charlotte was; he should've made a point of arranging a meeting point.

"Hi, Gage."

He whirled around, the greeting he had lodged in his throat. Wearing a pale blue halter dress that stopped just above her knees, Charlotte looked like a sexy goddess. Her hair was loose and covered her shoulders, the glossy strands glowing in the sunlight. If he didn't have his hands full of food and drinks, he would have run his fingers through it to see if it was as soft as it looked.

"Hey. You look lovely. That color suits you."

He could tell he'd surprised her by the way her green eyes widened. Hell, he'd surprised himself.

"Uh, thank you." She nodded toward the brown paper bag he held and the drinks in the cardboard holder. "And you got food. I brought a blanket."

"Okay, let's find somewhere to sit."

"That works."

He headed down the steps and made his way across the grass, where he found a space beneath a tree. Within seconds Charlotte had the blanket laid out.

"What food did you get?"

Gage kneeled down and placed the bag of food and the drink container in the middle of the blanket.

"I wasn't sure what you liked, but I figured I couldn't go wrong with a garden salad and some fried chicken. As for drinks, I played it safe and got you a Diet Coke and myself an iced tea."

"Oh … Diet Coke."

"What? You don't like Diet Coke?"

Charlotte shook her head. "I don't like diet sodas."

"You must be the only girl I know who doesn't like diet drinks. Would you like the iced tea then?"

"Is that okay?"

"Sure. I don't mind Diet Coke."

"Thanks."

He opened the containers of food and handed Charlotte one of the plates the café had supplied to go with their lunch, then watched as she filled it up. It was nice to see a woman put a decent amount of food on her plate. The last couple of dates he'd been on before his dad died would've freaked if he'd turned up with fried chicken.

They ate in silence for a few minutes.

"You know, there really is no cute way to eat fried chicken," Charlotte said conversationally.

"Sometimes the best-tasting food can't be eaten pretty."

"True. This is good, but it doesn't beat Betty Lou's fried chicken. That is the best chicken I've ever tasted. I suppose you've had it a ton of times?"

"No, I haven't. I never went there much."

"What? Why?"

He could understand her disbelief. It was a well-known fact that Betty Lou's was the place to go. He and his brothers and dad had just never gone.

"It's true. The Cooper family never went into the diner."

"But why?"

"The story I was told, Mom didn't like Betty Lou and demanded Dad not eat there. Dad is nothing but loyal, so he respected Mom's request and we never ate there. Even after she died, he never went there."

"Well, something changed. The first day I was in Sweet Ridge I had lunch there, and that's where I met Jack. He sat down and ate with me."

This revelation should've shocked Gage, but with the way his father had acted with regard to the will, it didn't. It made total sense Jack would've started to frequent the diner. Everything his father had done the last few months of his life seemed out of character.

"Well, we'll never know his reasons for his change of heart."

"You miss him, don't you?"

How did he answer that? He had a lot of regrets where his relationship with his father was concerned. If only they'd had a little more time to fully resolve their issues. Although before he died, Dad seemed to give the impression that all was forgiven. Maybe he'd been wrong and Dad hadn't completely forgiven and forgotten Gage's mistakes.

"I guess I do. I wish I'd said a few more things to him. Explained why I'd done the things I did."

"Life is always full of regrets. Sometimes you have to accept that, no matter how hard it is."

Gage shrugged. In principle, acceptance seemed the logical course of action. In reality, forgiving himself for his shortcomings wasn't something he could do.

"Do you have any regrets, Charlotte?" He turned the question on her to take the heat off him.

"I think I do."

"What do you mean, you think you do? Either you do or you don't."

"Well, I regret not being more open with some of the kids I met on my dad's various overseas assignments. As an ex-pat kid, it's better not to get too attached to the people you associate with. As you said, contracts end. You move on to another school. Another group of people. Another place to call home for a couple of years."

He had always thought of traveling as an exciting prospect. Until he started working on the oil rigs. He'd worked on some all over the world, and soon tired of living out of a suitcase. He'd been glad when his investments had paid off and he could buy a fifty percent share of the company that had hired him. The timing had been perfect, and he never looked back. After a year of becoming a part owner of the company, he'd taken full ownership when his partner wanted out due to ill health. The fact that Gage was twenty-five at that time had been an achievement within itself.

"So, where is home for you?"

"At the moment it's here in Houston."

"But you'd like to make it Sweet Ridge?"

Sadness etched its way over her features. "I thought it could be…" she whispered, "more of a weekend getaway."

"And it can't be now?"

"No, it doesn't seem likely."

"Why?" God, couldn't she give him straight answers instead of riddles to solve?

"It's a bit far to travel from Australia to Sweet Ridge just for a weekend jaunt."

Gage sat back and reviewed the conversation they'd had the last time they were together. She'd mentioned something about a green card and her company sponsoring her. Had that fallen through? Or had they changed their mind? He couldn't believe Charlotte had changed her mind about living in Houston. Not with the way she was acting.

"What happened, Red?"

"My company investigated the green card process and decided against proceeding with the application. While they wanted to employ me on a permanent basis, last week they got the news they'd missed out on two contracts they bid on. The application cost, while not too prohibitive, was more than they wanted to spend. So when my contract ends in a couple of months, I'll be heading back home."

"I'm sorry. I know you were excited about the prospect of staying. But why would you want to live here? From everything I've heard and from other people I've talked to, most people would give their eyeteeth to live in Australia."

"I mean, it is beautiful. I love going back there, but because I've traveled so much, it hasn't really felt like home. I seem to have inherited my parents' need to experience new things and places. My brothers, on the other hand, are quite content to settle down in Australia. They've started their own company, so they've got no plans to leave."

"But why here? What's so special about Houston? It's not exactly pretty, if you know what I mean."

"It may not have a beautiful harbor like Sydney or the gorgeous Blue Mountains. But Houston has a vibe all its own. It's cosmopolitan. It has great restaurants. Brilliant shopping. There's just something about the place that appeals to me. Maybe it's the international feel with so many ex-pats living here." She shrugged. "I really can't say why I like it here, I just do."

"So, what are you going to do?"

"I spent some time looking into ways to get a green card myself, but it's impossible. To work here, you have to have a company backing you. And even though Gold Star Eco wants me to stay, it's just not a feasible thing for them at the moment. Their business relies on contracts. If they start to get outbid on more contracts like they did on these last few, or if contract opportunities peter out with the price of oil dropping, then they'll be laying people off."

"Tell me about it," he muttered. "I'm sure there are other options. Maybe look for another job?"

Charlotte arched one of her auburn eyebrows. "Are you hiring?"

"No, although having you on my team might mean you won't oppose everything the company does and make my life a lot easier."

"Don't count on it, Cowboy. I'd probably be tougher on you."

"Yeah, you probably would." He took a sip of his drink. "And there really aren't any other options?"

"Nope. Pity I wasn't on that reality show *90-Day Fiancée*."

Gage spat out his drink. "What is that show?"

Charlotte blushed, the light pink infusing her face. He quite liked seeing her uncomfortable. "It's a show where people bring their girlfriends or boyfriends over from another country and then they have to get married after ninety days or they get sent back."

"Now I've heard everything. Charlotte Wilkinson is a closet reality TV junkie."

"Not quite. I was clicking through the channels one Sunday night and came across it. I watched one episode, but like everything else when it comes to reality television, it was probably scripted."

"I guess if they live in a country where opportunities are limited, marrying to get a green card seems like the perfect idea for them."

"If someone is desperate, they'll do anything for a chance at changing their fate."

"So we've gotten a little off-topic, but what do you plan to do about the land, then?"

"I guess I'll sell it to you when the year is up."

The sadness crept back into her voice and demeanor. While he wanted the land badly, he'd seen the excitement on Charlotte's face at the old house last weekend. She really did want the property, too. And with the way she spoke about her love for travel, she wouldn't stay in Australia long. Which made him wonder why she thought she would stay in the United States permanently. No doubt the wanderlust would hit her again and she'd sell everything she owned and flit off to some other place. He'd probably never get his hands on the land if that happened.

"I'll pay you above market price for the land when the time comes."

Or you could marry her and get the land via marriage instead of paying an absurd amount for it.

Gage shushed the voice in his mind. It was the most ridiculous idea he'd had, and it didn't warrant a second thought.

And he wasn't going to fall into the same trap Gavin did with Macy and end up in love. Who fell in love within a few weeks? But they had a history where animosity disguised their true feelings. Gavin had always had a crush on Macy. He and Charlotte had no history. Their animosity was work-related, and no emotions came into the equation at all.

Make it a business deal. Propose marriage and you could have everything you want. The land, the oil, and she gets her green card.

The absurd thought wouldn't leave his mind. The last time he'd let that voice control his thoughts, though, he'd been kicked out of college. He'd learned long ago nothing good came from listening to it.

Chapter 8

A knock at her door made Charlotte look up from the environmental report she'd been attempting to read. She welcomed the interruption. While she should've been taking in the levels of contaminates in the soil, her mind had been on the prospect of finding another job. Where, she didn't know. She needed to make a plan. But she really didn't want to. She wanted to stay here. She liked working for Gold Star and she enjoyed Houston.

"What's up, Meredith?"

"Gage Cooper is here to see you. I don't have him listed for an appointment."

Of course, Gage would just turn up without an appointment.

"That's fine. I need a break from this report anyway. Send him in."

"Okay."

Charlotte closed the report and placed it in her in-tray. She put her pen in the penholder. The door opened and Gage filled her doorway, dressed casually in blue jeans, white button-down shirt with a cowboy hat on his head and, even though she couldn't see his feet, she would bet a month's salary he had on cowboy boots.

He looked like he would be as comfortable on the back of a horse as he no doubt was in the oil field.

"Good morning, Gage. What are—" She stopped when a flash of black landed on her desk. "And Oil Slick, too. What you both doing here?"

"Damn cat refuses to be left by herself in the condo. If I don't want to come home to a shredded pillow or couch, she has to come with me."

The image of big, strong Gage walking into his office with a cat on a lead was a sight she needed to see. "Do you take her to all your meetings? I'm sure that must go over well."

He moved into the room and closed the door before he took a seat. "No, I don't. She usually stays in the office with my assistant. Trailing a cat on a lead doesn't help my image as a tough-nosed businessman."

"So you don't need to make that impression with me?" She patted the cat, who started purring before she curled up in the middle of her desk.

"Red, you know when it comes to our business relationship, you are the one who is tough-nosed. Not me."

Charlotte shook her head. "I don't know whether I've just been complimented or insulted."

"Definitely complimented."

"Really? That surprises me."

"While I may not agree with everything you say, or rather, suggest, I appreciate someone who is passionate about their job. And you are very passionate."

Again, she wasn't entirely sure what to make of that comment. It seemed genuine, and he was right. She was passionate about her job. When her father had a year-long assignment in Brazil, she'd been fascinated by the rainforests and jungle. Her love for maintaining the integrity of the environment became her goal in life. So while she appreciated that mining for any sort of mineral was necessary, there were ways it could be done without compromising the environment.

Unfortunately, for so many years Gage and his ilk had only concerned themselves with getting the oil out of the ground and not with taking care of the land. Of course they disliked her when she came along and held them accountable for their actions.

"Well, thank you. So, to what do I owe this surprise visit from you and Oil Slick?"

As if a shutter had been pulled down over a window, blocking out the bright sunshine, Gage's temperament went from light to dark. She sat a little straighter.

"I've been thinking about our get-together last weekend."

"What about it?"

"It's to do with the land."

Bloody hell, not the land again. Why did he need to talk about it continually? The wheels were in motion for him to obtain the land in just over a year. The way time flew, it would be here before he knew it.

"I don't think we have much more to talk about, do we? You're getting what you want."

"I know, but I feel I need to be honest with you about the real reasons I want the land."

Huh? What did he mean, the "real reasons"?

"Gage, you've made it more than clear. Jack promised he would leave it to you when he died. For reasons unknown to anyone, Jack changed his will and left it to me. What more is there to know?"

"You remember when you were looking at the house and I told you I wanted to walk the perimeter again?"

"Yes."

"Well, the reason I wanted to do it, is because Dad had the land surveyed years ago and found a pocket of oil."

As irrational as it seemed, considering her expertise in the business, emotion overtook her sensibilities and all Charlotte could see in her mind was the quaint little house being demolished to make way for rod pumps and storage tanks. The woodland surrounding the property would no doubt be cleared, as well. How many animals would be left without a home? How many plants destroyed?

"You do realize you've taken a big risk in telling me this, don't you? I don't have to sell the land to you. Or I could sell the land to you and keep the mineral rights. Because those are what you're really after, aren't they? You don't care about the house or the land, just what's buried deep below."

"Yes, I knew coming here to let you know my real reasons for wanting the land would probably not work in my favor. But I need to be honest with you."

"I don't understand this, Gage. You've basically killed any hope of you getting the land by telling me your plans. You know what I do for a living. You know I've been fighting with your company to at least try to protect the environment around your rigs. To work on plans to rehabilitate the land after you've finished drilling."

"Yes, I understand all of that, and while it doesn't make sense, maybe it will if I tell you the other reason why I'm here."

This meeting had turned into something surreal. The man in front of her wasn't acting like the astute businessman she knew him to be. Why would he all but shoot himself in the foot with his declaration?

"Lay it on me. I'm sure it can't be any stranger than what you've already told me."

Gage leaned over the table and picked up the cat, the little animal mewling in disgust at being woken from its comfortable perch on her desk. "I think we should get married."

Now Charlotte knew for sure she'd misheard Gage, even though her heart rate increased at the idea. "I'm sorry, you did not just say that we should get married. That's the most absurd idea I've ever heard. We hardly know each other. We haven't even been on a proper date. And I don't count our lunch over the weekend as a date."

"I know it seems a bit out of left field, but think about it. Marrying would solve all of our problems."

Charlotte couldn't sit still; she pushed back from her desk and paced the small distance from her chair to the wall and back again. She glanced over at Gage; his eyes were a clear blue. No hint of anything to suggest his brain function might be impaired. Oil Slick looked up from her cozy position in Gage's arms, telling Charlotte she, too, could spend time in his warm embrace.

As if she'd want to do that. Perhaps *her* brain function was impaired if she imagined a cat encouraging her to take Gage up on his absurd suggestion.

"How on earth would marrying solve our problems?"

"You know how you talked about that show where couples have ninety days to decide if they want to get married?"

She looked at him cautiously. "Yes."

"Well, the idea hit me Saturday afternoon when we were together that this could be an option for you to stay in the States. I tried to ignore it, but I kept thinking about it. I went and looked on the federal immigration website. It looks like a really easy process to get a green card through marriage. So I decided to run with it."

"You decided to run with an idea that could—no wait, *will*—change our lives. Marriage isn't a game, you know. When I marry it will be for love and once only."

"Just hear me out, okay? If you say no that's fine, but you have to admit the idea is intriguing." He flashed a sexy smile and Charlotte's gaze was drawn back to where the cat still sat.

"Intriguing? No. A stupid idea? Yes. But fine, I'll hear you out." She sat back down behind her desk. "It doesn't mean I'm going to agree."

"Fair enough. As I was saying, it doesn't appear to be a difficult process, according to what I read on the website. We get married and then fill out the various forms necessary to apply for the green card."

"Are you sure? That seems too easy."

"Yep, it is. We may have to wait to get the initial approval, but that's fine. It's not like we can do anything about transferring the land for twelve months anyway. The bonus is, by having the green card you'll be able to keep your job. I'm sure your employers will be happy about that. If they're not, you can easily find another job with your experience. Also, you can work with me through the whole process of getting the land surveyed and all that we have to do to commence the drilling process. I'm not going to start drilling tomorrow. I'm going to wait until oil is at a better price. We can split up a year after we get married. You'll have your green card then, so you can go anywhere. Get a job in another state. As part of the divorce settlement, I'll make sure you get a portion of the profits when I start drilling the oil. Those funds alone could mean you probably won't have to work ever again. You'll be able to travel to your heart's content. What do you think?"

The more he talked, the more excited he got. She knew it wasn't excitement about marrying her, but more about owning the land and what was beneath the topsoil. And the prospect of fattening of his already fat bank account.

"I think you're insane. This whole conversation is unbelievable. Didn't you hear me when I said I only wanted to get married once—and only for love?"

"Sure, I heard that, but this would be a purely business arrangement, not a love match. A sale contract, you could say. You get a green card. I get the land. No hearts involved at all."

Charlotte laughed at that suggestion.

"What if I don't want you to do anything to the land until after I'm gone? Will that be a problem?"

"As I said, with the price of oil so low at the moment I'm more than happy to wait until it improves before we begin the process of setting everything up and then bringing in the equipment to dig the wells, etc."

"No, what I'm saying here is, what if I don't want you to do a survey? No touching it until I no longer have any real vested interest in the land."

While some might have thought she was being difficult, for her it was more about hoping that maybe, just maybe, Gage would see there was more to the land than oil.

Yeah, like that would ever happen, and judging by the frown on his face, he wasn't happy with her suggestion to hold off.

"I don't see why we have to wait."

"It's my land, Gage. Not yours. That's the only reason you need to understand."

"Fine." He huffed and crossed his arms over his chest.

"So the marriage would be a business arrangement only. No sleeping together. Nothing like that."

"I would think there would be times when we would have to hold hands and maybe kiss. But yes, it would be solely a business arrangement."

Charlotte nodded. That would work. It wouldn't be a hardship to hold hands and occasionally kiss Gage. He was a good-looking guy, and she was slightly attracted to him. No, the issue would be living with him. Being around him and his ego twenty-four/seven.

God, was she really considering his idea? It would mean she could stay in the States indefinitely. And did it really matter if she blotted her life's copybook with a divorce? It's not as if it was frowned upon these days.

As proposals went, it was the most unromantic she could imagine, but yes, she really was considering this idea.

"Well, as I said earlier, I think you're insane, and I'm obviously crazy, too, because I'm saying yes. Yes, Gage Cooper, I will marry you."

Chapter 9

Gage checked his watch again. He should've insisted on picking Charlotte up. For goodness' sake, they lived less than four blocks apart from each other, but she insisted on making her own way to the airport. Or he should've suggested they take his personal jet instead of a flight on a domestic carrier. He'd been reluctant to mention to her that he had his own jet. He didn't want to seem too arrogant. Now he kind of wished he had.

As the time ticked away, he began to wonder whether she had developed cold feet and decided not to marry him after all. His phone beeped and he pulled it out of his pocket. Maybe it was a text message from Charlotte, canceling. Nope. Just a text from the surveyor saying he'd received the measurements he'd sent and would arrange the survey when Gage told him to.

"I'm so sorry I'm late. The security line was a nightmare."

Gage jumped and shoved the phone in his pocket. In a whirlwind of motion, so unlike the organized Charlotte he knew, she sat down in the seat next to him. Her sweet, flowery perfume enveloped him, and he took a deep breath.

"It's okay. I wasn't worried."

"Liar." She rolled her eyes. "I saw you glancing at your watch and fiddling with your phone. Your leg was bouncing up and down. You thought I had second thoughts, didn't you?"

If she could tell when her brothers were lying, Gage knew there would be no point in trying to evade the truth.

"Fine, yes. The thought crossed my mind that you were having second thoughts. Can you blame me? You're cutting it a bit close."

"Hey, I'm not the one who changed our plans twice. At the last minute, too, I might add. I should be asking *you* if you're having second thoughts."

Shit, how did he handle this? He wasn't having second thoughts. Why would he? In twelve months' time he was going to get everything he wanted. He needed to make plans, and the people he wanted to speak to had been away. He could've waited until after the wedding, of course, but he wanted his plans sorted out before he and Charlotte tied the knot. And one of those had just been confirmed with the text message.

"No second thoughts here. I had some issues at work I needed to sort out."

"Is everything okay?"

He was saved from answering when the boarding call for their flight to Vegas sounded over the loudspeaker.

He heard the sharp intake of breath and looked over at her. Charlotte was clutching her bag, her fingers white around the straps. "Are you sure you want to go to Vegas to do this? We could just stay here and go to the registry office. I'm sure Gavin and Macy would be more than happy to act as our witnesses," he asked.

She shook her head and put her hand on his arm. Immediately his body flared to life, like solar flares shooting out from the sun. "I've never admitted this to anyone. But I kind of dig the idea of getting married in Vegas. It just seems so much fun."

"Well, then," he said, standing and holding out his hand. "Let's go."

• • •

The car pulled to a stop at the front of the Hotel Bellagio. The fountains danced merrily in an exuberant greeting.

"Whoa, this is amazing," Charlotte said as she got out of the car. She had to pinch herself to believe she actually stood in the driveway of a Vegas hotel.

"It really is a sight to behold at night. I'll make sure you get to see the full show, but first we've got a chapel to get to."

Butterflies scurried to life in her belly. She had no idea why she felt so nervous. She could understand if this was a wedding she'd spent months planning. But it had been just a couple of weeks since Gage proposed the idea of marriage. Now here they were, about to embark on a new journey together.

God, could she sound any cheesier? They weren't embarking on anything but a business deal.

"Okay, I'll hold you to that. Let's go."

Gage steered her toward the lobby, which was as opulent as she expected a Vegas hotel foyer to be. She wasn't a gambler, but the noise from the casino drifted out—bells ringing, signaling a jackpot win, people yelling in excitement as their number came up on the craps table—tempting her to experience the essence of Las Vegas.

"Can we go to the casino later on?" she asked.

"Sure, although I wouldn't have pegged you as someone who likes to dabble on the tables."

"I don't normally, but what happens in Vegas stays in Vegas, right?"

"Yep. Why don't you wait here while I go check us in?"

As he walked away, a sliver of panic fought for supremacy over the nervous butterflies currently occupying her stomach. She hadn't thought to ask Gage if they would have separate rooms. He had better have booked separate rooms; otherwise they'd have a very short marriage. No way would he assume that just because he put a ring on it, she'd change her mind about sleeping with him. Would he?

Moments later, Gage returned to her side.

"You look like you are having a fight with yourself and neither side is winning."

"Nope. No fighting. And besides, I always win."

He looked at her quizzically, and she expected him to question her further. Instead he shrugged his shoulders in an *I'll-never-understand-women* motion.

"Right, well, how about we go to our rooms? It's almost one and we have to be at the chapel by four thirty. Will that give you enough time to get ready?"

"That should be plenty of time."

Gage cupped her elbow, then effortlessly weaved them through the crowd to the bank of elevators.

Minutes later they were walking down the hallway toward their rooms.

They stopped outside of a door and Gage paused before inserting the key. "I asked for a suite, so that, you know, you could have a separate room to change into, and well—" Charlotte bit her lip to stop herself from laughing as pink stained his cheeks. It actually endeared him to her a little as he worked out what he was about to say next. "I remembered what you said about sleeping arrangements when you agreed to my proposal idea."

"Good." She inclined her head to the door. "How about you open the door and we can get ready for this business deal?"

"Works for me."

He inserted the key into the reader and opened the door, allowing her to precede him into the room.

It was like they'd entered a small apartment. There was a decent-sized foyer before it opened into a large living room. The back of the room was made up completely of windows, and with the blinds open the Strip was presented before her in all its glory. She couldn't wait to see what it looked like at night.

"Pretty spectacular, isn't it?"

She was so caught up in the view, she'd momentarily forgotten Gage was in the room with her. "Oh, it is. How many times have you been to Vegas?"

"I've been here a couple of times. A long time ago." A shadow passed over his face. What had happened?

"Don't tell me your trip was like the one in *The Hangover*. You look like you still have all your teeth," she joked.

It brought a wry smile to his face. "Not quite, although when I got home … well, let's just say that Vegas and I haven't had the best of relationships."

Emotions played across Gage's face. The man seemed to have so many secrets. If they were in a real relationship, she'd ask him to expand further. But they weren't, and learning about Gage's past wasn't part of the deal.

"Let's hope this trip will improve that relationship a little. I can assure you I don't know anybody here with a pet tiger."

"Good to know. Why don't you pick a room?"

Charlotte went to walk away, stopping when Gage touched her arm.

"I know this probably isn't the wedding day you dreamed of, getting married without your family here," he said quietly. "If you want, we can plan a big party later, either in Sweet Ridge or in Houston."

Perhaps Jack *had* taught his sons some manners along the way. Only an ice queen would miss the sincerity of Gage's offer. "Thank you. I have to admit, I wasn't a girl who pored over wedding magazines or dreamed about my big day. We can do a party in Sweet Ridge if you'd like. And it's okay that my family's not here. It's not like this is a real wedding, is it?"

"Geez, here I am trying to help you and make you feel comfortable with our arrangement, and you go and make a bitchy comment like that."

Normally being called "bitchy" would've sent her temper steaming to the boiling point. On this occasion, however, she deserved it. Gage was trying to be a gentleman toward her, an action she hadn't expected. Business marriage or not, she didn't want it to start off on the wrong foot.

"I'm sorry, Gage. You're right, my comment was uncalled for."

"Actually, it's probably a good reminder of where we stand in this whole arrangement. If you still want to go ahead with it, I'll leave you to get ready."

Charlotte sighed, all humor gone from their conversation. "Yes, I still want to get married."

He nodded before heading toward one of the bedrooms that led off the main living room. "Fine. I arranged for a car to arrive downstairs at four so it can take you to the chapel."

Take *her* to the chapel? What about him? "You're not coming with me?"

"No." He shrugged his shoulders. "As unconventional as the whole basis of our getting married is, I wanted to give you as much of a real wedding experience as possible. So, in line with wedding traditions, I don't want to see my bride until she's walking down the aisle toward me."

Charlotte's mouth dropped open. Never in a million years would she have guessed that the brash, arrogant, accusatory Gage Cooper gave a damn about wedding traditions. She couldn't deny that if he continued these sorts of thoughtful actions, she could fall for him—and that would be extremely dangerous. The plan was to split after a year. She couldn't let these wonderful gestures cloud her end goal.

"Umm, thank you."

Clearing his throat, he continued on his way to his room. "Guess the next time I see you will be at the chapel."

"Yep, I'll be there."

Chapter 10

Charlotte checked her purse one last time to ensure the ring she'd purchased for Gage was safely ensconced in the inside pocket as the car made its way down the road toward the wedding chapel. They hadn't discussed wedding rings; she would give him the option of wearing it, and if he decided he didn't want to, she'd deal with returning the ring when she got back to Houston.

But she hoped he would, and that he'd like it.

"Here we are." The driver's voice broke through her thoughts.

The cute white chapel didn't look tacky—it looked more like an old-fashioned church you might find in a small country town. Gage had chosen well.

Her door was opened for her and she stepped out, taking the hand the driver extended, making sure he didn't step on her long dress. Her initial plan had been to get something simple, a dress she could wear again if necessary. That plan had changed. The moment Charlotte had seen this dress in the bridal boutique window down the street from her apartment, she knew it was perfect for her. The strapless dress had a sweetheart neckline that hinted at cleavage without being too "in your face." It fell in a straight column until it fanned out just below her knees. The woman in the store had called it a mermaid-style dress. Charlotte didn't care—she only knew that once she had it on, she knew it was her dress.

Now she adjusted the crystal-encrusted belt that matched the headband in her hair. Her drop diamanté earrings kissed her cheek when she moved her head. She wore her mother's diamond necklace to finish the outfit. She felt elegant ... like a bride.

The driver walked her up the path, and someone held open the door to the chapel for her.

"Ahh, here's our bride," an older woman gushed. "I'm Ruth, and welcome to Ruth and Phil's Wedding Chapel."

Charlotte noticed they were in a reception area. Gage was nowhere to be seen. He was here, wasn't he?

As if sensing her question, Ruth clucked her tongue. "Don't you worry, dear. Your man is through those doors there, and he's looking as nervous as you."

A little giggle erupted from Charlotte, startling her—she never giggled. She took a deep breath to get her emotions under control. "Right, thanks. So, umm, do I just go through?" she asked.

"Not yet, dear. Let's let him sweat for a little bit. Besides, you need a bouquet before you go in there. Can't get married without one. Now, come with me and I'll show you what we have available."

Ruth took her by the arm and led her to a small area where various flower bouquets rested in small glass vases. There were bouquets of roses and lilies, roses only, lilies only—so many to choose from. Finally, she settled on a posy of brightly colored spring flowers.

"Perfect choice. Now, are you ready to get married?"

The enormity of what was about to happen suddenly hit her. When she walked through those double doors, she would be saying good-bye to her single life. Whether the marriage was for convenience or for love—her and Gage's lives was about to change.

Was she ready for that? Was she ready to share a space with a man she'd known for less than a month and could say she'd only liked for about fifteen minutes during that time?

The door opened and a man stepped out. Before the door shut she caught sight of Gage's back. He wore a black suit, and he was checking his watch. She smiled.

Yes.

Yes, she was ready to do whatever it took to get a green card.

"Are you ready here, Ruth?" the man who walked through the door asked.

"Just a minute, Phil." Ruth turned to Charlotte. "You alright, dear?"

"Yes." Perhaps the more times she said yes, the more times she'd convince herself it would all be worth it in the end.

"Splendid," Phil said. "I'll get back inside to the anxious groom."

The butterflies from earlier migrated back into her stomach as the sound of Wagner's "Wedding March" filled the chapel. The doors were flung open, and Charlotte took a small step until she stood on the threshold between the foyer and the wedding sanctuary.

Gage turned around, a serious look on his face. His eyes widened as he took in her appearance, and a slow, sexy smile broke out across his face. He mouthed the word "*wow*" as she started her measured walk down the aisle.

Their eyes never left each other, and to anyone observing, they probably looked like they were in love. Maybe they could pull off the whole in-love thing after all, convince Gage's family and hers that this was a match made in heaven, and not a match made in an office. The moment she reached his side, Gage slipped his arm through one of hers.

"You look breathtaking," he whispered in her ear.

It was impossible to hold back the ripple of awareness storming through her body.

"So do you." The image of Gage in a tuxedo would be permanently imprinted on her mind. He looked even better in his tux in real life than he had in the dream she'd had after they'd danced at the Silver Spurs.

"Are you two ready?" asked Phil.

"Yes," they responded simultaneously.

The next few minutes passed in a blur for Charlotte. She responded when she was supposed to. Repeated vows when asked.

"Do you both have rings you'd like to exchange?" Phil asked.

"I do," Gage replied.

"Umm, so do I."

Because they were holding hands facing each other, she couldn't miss Gage's surprise.

She cleared her throat. "But if you don't want to wear it, it's fine. I just thought…" She was unsure what to say next. She hadn't consciously thought she'd buy Gage a wedding band when she walked into the jewelers, but as she walked around the store she decided she would buy him one. She had been starting to lose hope of ever finding anything that would fit Gage's personality when she spied the acid-etched ring. With the whole center of the ring seeming to have been eaten away, it was rough but it had the smooth edges of a traditional band. She had arranged for a small black agate stone to be placed in the band. Black, to signify the color of the oil he worked so hard to find.

Gage squeezed her hands. "I'll be happy to wear it."

Phil and the chapel faded into the background, forgotten, as they looked at each other. Could Gage read the warring emotions in her eyes? It might have started out as a marriage ceremony for the express purpose of helping her obtain her green card, but with each passing minute it was becoming more and more real to her.

And it would be disastrous if she fell into that abyss. This was no fairy tale, where they'd wake up one morning and realize they'd been in love the whole time. No, this was an arrangement—an arrangement that would benefit the both of them.

She had no idea how long they stood there, holding hands, emotions and desires swirling between them.

"May I have the rings?" Phil asked.

"Oh, yes." Charlotte freed her hands from Gage's hold to get her purse where she'd placed it on the altar with her bouquet while she and Gage said their vows. With swift movements she opened the purse, extracted the ring, and placed it on the book Phil held out. Her breath caught at the sight of two other rings already resting on the pages.

Phil said a few words of blessing before he encouraged Gage to pick up the rings to place on her finger.

"Repeat after me, Gage. With these rings, I thee wed."

Gage slipped the diamond-encrusted band and diamond solitaire ring onto her finger. The central stone had to be at least two carats and was stunning. The fit was a little loose but not enough that they were going to slip off. She'd get them resized once she returned to Houston. "With these rings, I thee wed."

"Now, Charlotte, repeat after me. With this ring, I thee wed."

With shaking fingers she picked up Gage's ring. She really hoped she'd gotten the size right. The design of the ring didn't lend itself to being resized easily.

Breathing deeply, she said the words that sealed her fate and slid the ring home.

"By the power vested in me and the State of Nevada, I now pronounce you husband and wife. You may kiss your beautiful bride, Gage."

Oh God, the kiss. In the back of her mind, she'd known that they'd have to do this. How ironic that their first kiss was to be one that sealed their marriage. Would he kiss her on the cheek? On the lips? Would it be a short kiss or a long kiss? What if he kissed like a wet fish?

Gage closed the gap between them and cupped either side of her face. His touch warmed her cheeks.

"Hi, Mrs. Cooper," he whispered before he melded their lips together. He sipped slowly at her lips, encouraging her to open beneath him. The jolt of desire zipping through her took all sensible thought process away. Acting on instinct, she opened to let him in. As quickly as it started, though, the kiss was over, leaving her wanting more. More of his kisses. More of his touches. More Gage.

Shit, she would be in too deep if she let that happen. She had to keep it casual.

"Well, I have some documents for you to sign, and then I'll get Ruth to take some snaps for you so you have some happy memories. You make such a lovely couple."

Phil bustled off to get the necessary papers.

Charlotte touched the rings on her fingers, their weight a little foreign to her.

"I wasn't sure if you preferred a cluster setting or a solitaire. I ended up going for the solitaire because it looks elegant. I thought it would suit you better. If you don't like them, we can exchange them."

"Gage, they're beautiful. Far more than I expected to receive from you." She reached out and touched the ring she'd placed on his finger. "Same goes for you. I know you said you'd wear it, but if you'd prefer not to wear a ring, I'm okay with that. We didn't really talk about rings, did we?"

"I said it before, but in case you need to hear it again, I'm happy to wear the ring. It's different and I like different. What is the black stone?"

She moved back, breaking the contact between them. "It's black agate. I wanted to get something that symbolizes you." She briefly touched the smooth edge of the ring before running her finger over the rough surface. "Smooth on the outside, but complex on the inside. The stone is my way of acknowledging your passion for oil."

"I'm complex, am I?"

"Well, aren't we all? But yes, I do believe you are complex, and I've only seen the shiny surface. I've not seen the ragged depths that have molded you. I think there is so much more I could learn about you."

If her words upset him, he didn't show it. No one liked to have their character questioned, and while she didn't actually question him, she did truly sense there was something behind Gage's motivation to succeed. But did it really matter to her if she found out all his secrets?

A clearing of a throat behind them broke the spell surrounding them. Charlotte turned and saw Phil, papers in his hand.

"Time to get the formalities over and done with, and then you can begin your married life. Ruth has been taking photos, and let me say, she has got some lovely shots of you both. You can have your formal shots taken after we've dealt with this."

She looked over her shoulder; there in the corner stood Ruth with a digital camera in her hand. Charlotte had been so focused on Gage, she hadn't noticed.

"If you write down your e-mail addresses, I'll make sure to send you a link to them so you can download your favorites," Ruth offered.

A half hour later they walked outside, officially Mr. and Mrs. Gage Cooper.

The car that had driven her to the chapel was still parked out front, the driver leaning against it looking at his phone. He looked up when they approached and smiled.

"Congratulations," he commented as he opened the door. "Back to the hotel?"

"Thank you," Gage acknowledged. "And yes, back to the hotel."

The car had seemed so big when she'd been the only one in the backseat. With Gage occupying the seat next to her, the space appeared to reduce in size. It was a silly notion because the interior of the limo was spacious. But Gage's masculine energy pulsed around the space, filling it until it seemed like she was driving in one of those tiny smart cars.

All of a sudden it hit her: The last hour and a half hadn't been a dream. She really was married to a man she had nothing in common with.

Chapter 11

Gage's palms were sweaty as he reached into his pocket to extract the key to their suite. The concierge had seen them arrive, so by now the celebration dinner and champagne he'd ordered before he'd left for the chapel should be all set up on the balcony. Food would be resting in warming trays, champagne chilling in a bucket of ice.

"So, Mrs. Cooper, welcome to our little home away from home."

Mrs. Cooper.

That was the second time. He didn't know why he felt the need to reinforce their marital status by calling her that. Hell, she probably wouldn't even legally change her name. Why would she, when their marriage was only temporary?

"Thank you, and come to think of it, we haven't discussed our living arrangements yet, have we?"

That was true. They'd talked about flights and marriage license requirements, but they hadn't discussed what would happen after they tied the knot. He assumed they'd move into his condo together. He was sure Charlotte's company wasn't paying for her to live in a penthouse like he did.

"Let's talk about it on the flight home tomorrow. This is our wedding night. We're in Vegas. Let's enjoy ourselves."

Charlotte looked like she wanted to argue with him, but he placed a finger over her lips. "Later, Red. Besides, dinner is getting cold."

Taking her hand, he led her through the living room and entered his bedroom. He spoke before Charlotte could even say anything. "I'm not trying to be presumptuous. To get to our dinner location, we have to go through the bedroom."

"I believe you."

With a flourish he opened the balcony door. The sight that greeted them was more than what he'd expected. The staff had gone all out to make the dinner as romantic as possible.

"Wow, Gage, this is beautiful, and look at the Strip. It's so vibrant."

The table sat in the middle of the balcony, a white tablecloth covering it. In the center sat a small flower arrangement with a large pillar candle burning brightly. The silverware gleamed in the fading light of the setting sun.

He walked over to a seat and pulled it out. "Are you ready to eat?"

The fabric from her dress whispered seductively as she walked past him and sat. His body throbbed in anticipation of perhaps getting lucky enough to see what she had on beneath her gorgeous bridal dress. A foolish notion. There was no way he was going to get lucky for the next twelve months—unless he could get her to change her mind about the no sleeping together clause.

He sat opposite her and reached for the bottle of champagne to pour some into the flutes sitting on the table. Once he placed the bottle back in the bucket, he picked up his glass and held it high.

"You look beautiful, Charlotte, and your wedding dress is stunning. I'm a very lucky man. Here's to the beautiful woman I now get to call my wife."

He waited for Charlotte to raise her glass. She didn't. He lowered his glass. "Come on, Charlotte. I'm trying to make the best of the situation. Would you rather I raise a toast to hoping we don't kill each other in the next twelve months? It would be just as true."

"I don't know. What is going on between us, Gage?"

He blew out a breath. "The terms of our agreement haven't changed. We're married. The next step is getting you a green card."

"I understand all of that. But that toast … it seemed … well, too personal. It was a toast a man in love with his wife would say, not business partners."

"Well, we're not truly just business partners, are we? Charlotte, no matter what happens over the next twelve months between us, there are going to be situations where we're going to have to look like we love each other. Business dinners with prospective clients of mine. In front of my family. In front of your family. Do you want everyone to think we made a rash decision and that we can't stand each other?"

"Isn't that what we did? Didn't we just make a rash decision?"

Gage took a swallow of his champagne. He'd made plenty of rash decisions in the past. Decisions that had cost him his college education and football career. He didn't think this was one of them. He knew at the end of the day he was getting the land. He'd made plans on what he was going to do with that property. He'd wanted to do it while Dad was alive so he could see that his youngest son wasn't a loser. Now Dad was dead and his chance to prove his worth to him was gone. But it wasn't gone from proving to his brothers he wasn't just a punk kid who threw away a great opportunity when it presented itself.

"No, we didn't. We made a decision that would benefit the both of us. How about we toast to this instead?" He raised his champagne glass again. "To the both of us getting what we want."

He relaxed when Charlotte raised her glass and tapped it against his.

"Let's eat." Gage pushed back from the table and went over to the warming cart in the corner. Using a folded tea towel, he set a plate down in front of Charlotte before going back and getting his own.

As he cut into his steak, he remembered his first glimpse of Charlotte as she stood in the doorway of the chapel. He didn't know what he'd been expecting, but a wedding gown wasn't it. He'd been struck dumb by the way her dress hugged her every curve, and when she started walking toward him, he had to stop himself from striding down the aisle, scooping her up in his arms, and kissing her senseless. His instant reaction to her dressed as a bride baffled him. They merely tolerated each other. Their toast confirmed that. Still, he'd been very controlled with their first kiss as husband and wife. Their first kiss ever.

He glanced to his right, into the bedroom he'd chosen, and imagined Charlotte lying on the bed, waiting for him to possess her. He couldn't help it. He was a male having a dinner with an attractive female in a hotel room. Who wouldn't think of taking her to bed?

His body yelled at him to disregard the rest of the meal. He wanted to lift her from her chair and carry her over to the bed. But he wasn't going to go all Neanderthal on her.

"What are you thinking so hard about, Gage?"

"I'm not sure I should tell you."

"Really? You do know the rules now."

"Rules? What are these rules?"

"Being married, you have to tell me everything that goes on in your mind."

Gage leaned back in his chair and reached for his champagne again. "Is that so? I suppose if I have to tell you my every thought, then you have to do the same."

"Oh, no, that's not how it works. Only you have to bare your secrets. I pick and choose which ones I want to let you in on."

"That hardly seems fair."

"It is what it is. You should look it up in the rule book."

"I'll make sure I do that."

They finished the meal in silence, and once they were done he cleared away their dinner plates before replacing them with the dessert ones.

"Here you go." He lifted the lids to display matching bride and groom cupcakes. "It may not be fancy, but what is a wedding without wedding cake?"

"Please don't tell me you're going to smash this in my face. I don't get that tradition. It's not something we've ever done in Australia."

"Oh, I wouldn't dream of it. Why ruin a perfectly good cake by doing that? I'd much rather eat it. Although"—he smiled wickedly at her—"I'm all up for sharing."

"Settle down, Cowboy. I don't share my cake with anyone."

"Not even your brand-new husband?"

"Nope, not even with him."

"Maybe I will smash my cake in your face then," he mused.

She quirked an eyebrow and a challenging look entered her eyes. "You do recall me saying I have three brothers, don't you?"

He held his hands up, cupcake and all, in surrender. "Fine, forget I said that."

"Good." She was about to take a bite when he remembered something else.

"Wait, don't do anything yet."

Without waiting for a response, Gage strode into his bedroom, fished out his phone from the top drawer, and popped it into the holder in the top of the clock radio. A few seconds later music wafted through the room.

"Perfect," he murmured to himself as he walked back to the balcony and sat down. He picked up his cupcake and broke a bite off for Charlotte. "You want a taste?"

Instead of taking it from his fingers like he thought she would, she scooted her chair around so they were sitting side by side. He bit back a groan as her leg brushed his, sending the sparks of desire that he thought he had under control firing through him again. The temptation to take possession of her increased when she took the piece of the cake from his fingers and moaned in appreciation.

"This is good cake. Here, try mine." She repeated his action and held it out. Gage wrapped his fingers around her wrist and directed her hand toward his mouth. He kept his eyes locked with hers, satisfied with the way they opened wider when he took the cake she held out and swirled his tongue around her fingers.

Oh yes, perhaps Charlotte wasn't as immune to him as she thought she was. Maybe he could entice her to reconsider the boundaries she'd set down.

They continued to feed each other morsels of cake until a familiar tune played on his iPod. He grabbed a napkin, passed one to her, and wiped his hands.

"How about we dance?" he suggested.

Charlotte cocked her head and smiled at him when she recognized the tune. "This is Macy, isn't it?"

"Yep, and it's the song we danced to at the Silver Spurs. Seems appropriate we tick off another wedding tradition."

He pulled her into his embrace and started swaying to the music. There wasn't a lot of room on the balcony with the table set up there, but they made do. It was just nice to hold Charlotte in his arms again.

"You know something?" she mumbled against his neck.

"What?"

"You keep doing things like this, and I could almost believe you're a hopeless romantic."

"I'll let you in on a secret, Red."

"What's that?"

"I was channel-surfing the other night, and came across the movie *My Best Friend's Wedding*. I got my cues from there."

"Thank goodness for Julia Roberts, then."

"You know what else I discovered from watching that movie?"

"I'm afraid to ask"

"The bride and groom have to kiss on the dance floor."

He lowered his head and touched his lips to hers again. Her taste was sweet and tart from the cake and champagne. It was addictive and he wanted more. He trailed his hands down her back until they rested on the curve of her ass. He pulled her a little tighter in his arms, so there was not an inch of space between them as his mouth roved over hers. Her mouth opened beneath his. He swallowed her moan of pleasure as his hand moved from her ass up to the underside of her breast. He pushed his hips into her, blatantly announcing how much he wanted her.

He broke their connection, his breath coming in harsh, rapid pants. "Can you feel how much I want you? It doesn't make sense to me. I don't know if it makes sense to you. Let me make love to you, Charlotte."

Gage knew he'd pushed too far the moment she pulled herself out of his embrace.

"This is all happening a bit too fast for me. I can't do it. I'm sorry."

If he let his disappointment show after that shoot-down, he'd look like he wanted her for only one thing. No guy was dumb enough to announce that, especially not when he needed his wife's land. Gage pulled her back into his embrace and kissed the top of her head, like he didn't mind in the least.

"Perhaps I was getting caught up in the whole things-to-do-on-your-wedding-day list."

Charlotte laughed like he hoped she would.

"It's still early—do you want to check out the casino? I mean, it's not like Vegas will be going to sleep at ten at night like some of the establishments in Sweet Ridge."

"You really want to get the whole Vegas experience while you're here?"

"I'm not sure when I'll ever get back."

"Sure, why not." He pointed to her dress. "Do you want to change?"

"Yep. I'll be back in a few minutes."

He nodded as Charlotte walked away, grateful he would have a few minutes to get his mind off taking her to bed. He wouldn't give up, though.

Twelve months was a long time to be celibate.

Chapter 12

She took a deep breath before raising her fist to knock on the door to Allen's office. The light glinted off the stunning diamond rings adorning her finger. She still couldn't believe the amount of money Gage had spent on her wedding rings.

"Come in," Allen called through the door.

"Hi, Allen," she said as she strode into the office. "I hope you had a good weekend."

"Good morning, Charlotte. How are you?"

"I'm great, and I've got some news I hope will please you. May I sit?"

"Certainly, take a seat."

She sat in one of the chairs on the other side of his desk. "I wanted to let you know that I got married over the weekend."

He sat forward, clearly shocked by her announcement. "Married? Well, congratulations, that's wonderful. Who's the lucky man?"

This was where it got tricky. Gage was a client, and although there wasn't a written rule about fraternization between staff and clients, she wanted to get everything on the table.

"Gage Cooper."

"That name rings a bell. Do I know him?"

"In a roundabout sort of way. He's the owner of Cooper Oil. We've had some dealings with him."

Allen tapped a finger against his lips. "Well, now, this could present a problem."

Crap, this was what she'd been concerned about. It was only on the flight back from Vegas that the thought hit her: there could be consequences from her marriage to Gage when it came to her employment. And those issues didn't have anything to do with her now being able to get a green card.

"I want to assure you, Allen, that just because Gage is my husband, he will in no way influence me when it comes to working on issues that come up in relation to his company."

"That may be true, but I'm still uneasy about this. Marriage to a client is something we've never come across before. It may not be an issue, though, with your contract finishing up soon. Although I'm disappointed we were unable to follow through with our idea of applying for a green card for you, with this latest news it's probably best we aren't proceeding with it."

A sinking feeling of dread filled Charlotte. The only reason she'd gotten married was so she could stay employed with Gold Star Eco. The way Allen was talking, however, even though she could now apply for a green card, they were still ready to let her go at the end of her contract—but for another reason: her marriage to Gage.

"That's another thing. Now that I'm married, I will be applying to stay in the US permanently. I'm hoping the suggestion you initially made about me taking up a permanent position with Gold Star is still open. I'd like to stay with the company, if possible."

Allen placed his hand on his table. "That is good news, and something I will have to bring up with the board. We have started to consider other alternatives, though. In the meantime, I think it might be best if we redirect you to other projects we've got in the pipeline."

While it wasn't confirmation that her employment was safe, it was a small concession. She didn't know what she'd do if she lost her job. "Thank you, Allen. And I understand your position with my new marital status. I'll look forward to the new projects."

She made a hasty retreat and refrained from slapping the wall on the other side of Allen's office. Why hadn't she investigated all the angles to this harebrained plan of theirs? Now she could have a dismissal *and* a divorce on her record.

But it was still possible she'd wind up with the job she loved and a man she didn't.

She made it to her office and fired up her laptop, going through her list of things to do. The first item was going back to the federal immigration website to download the forms needed for her green card application. The page concerning green card applications through marriage was just as Gage had said—get married, complete the forms. She had meant to go back and look further, but a minor accident at one of their client's rigs had necessitated meeting after meeting to contain the oil spill and start the cleanup process. All those lost plants and animals covered in oil. This was why she was so passionate about implementing measures to protect the surrounding land, although she didn't have all the answers to protecting the environment from accidents. She'd gotten home each night and collapsed, too exhausted to even watch television, let alone unravel the mysteries of the US immigration procedures.

Her door burst open and Meredith stood in the doorway. "Is it true?"

"Good morning, Meredith, and is what true?"

Her assistant moved into her office and closed the door. "The news I've just heard. I was in Allen's office and he told me to give you the Clarke folders and give Lester the Cooper files because you're now married to Gage Cooper."

Charlotte had hoped the news wouldn't spread so quickly, but there was no point in denying it.

"It's true. I married Gage in Vegas this weekend."

"Oh my goodness! I had no idea you were seeing him. I mean, he came to your office twice, but I thought they were work-related visits, not personal. If I didn't like you so much, I'd be angry that you've managed to snag one of Houston's most eligible bachelors."

Charlotte couldn't help but laugh at Meredith's enthusiasm. It was either that or cry from the stress of having to answer questions so soon. Here was her first test in convincing people the validity of her and Gage's relationship. But she also didn't know what to say to her assistant exactly. She couldn't blurt out that she'd married Gage just so she could get a green card. She wanted to keep that as quiet as possible. Better to embellish the relationship a little, make it seem to her coworkers that it was a true love match. "It was kind of a spur-of-the-moment thing. You know how it is with whirlwind romances. One minute we were talking about my idea to introduce a regrowth plan at one of his drilling sites, and the next minute he proposed. I knew the first time I saw Gage that he was the one for me, so it really wasn't a hard decision to accept his proposal."

"Oh, how romantic. Show me your ring," Meredith demanded.

Yep, she deserved an acting award. Charlotte held out her hand.

"Holy cow, that set is beautiful. It suits you perfectly. Did you pick it out yourself?"

"No, Gage did."

"Girl, he has good taste. You'd better hang on to that man," she finished wistfully. "Anyway, I'd better get back to my work. When you've got all the files together, can you please let me know? I'll come get them."

"Will do."

But she was talking to a closed door. She sat back in her chair and looked at the rings on her finger. It still amazed her that Gage had picked out something that suited her so well.

Her phone buzzed with an incoming text. She picked it up and saw Gage's name before the screen faded to black.

Unlocking her phone, she pulled up the message.

Hey Red,

I hope you're having a good morning. I thought I'd pick you up from work and then we can go to your place and collect your stuff. Let me know if that works.

G

The trip to her place wasn't necessary. She'd not collected too many extra things beyond what she'd brought with her when she moved overseas. She'd packed up her things last night after Gage had dropped her off at her apartment, and she currently had three suitcases and two boxes of belongings sitting in her car.

Kissing Gage on the balcony and almost falling under the spell he had created with all the special wedding day touches, meant she'd spent a sleepless wedding night knowing he was just a few feet away in a room by himself. Then their plane had been delayed out of Vegas, so she'd asked if she could spend the night at her place when they finally got home. She had expected Gage to put up a fight, but he'd agreed. Perhaps he needed a night to himself, as well.

She knew he wouldn't have objected if she walked into his room in the hotel suite and climbed into bed with him. But getting involved with Gage in a sexual way would only complicate their arrangement. Still, though, she did want him. She'd have to be made of ice not to appreciate his good looks. His toned, hard body. The way he kissed.

And now she was moving into his condo.

She quickly typed a message back to let him know that she would meet him at his place.

Her phone buzzed again and a "K" showed up on the screen. A man of few words.

She answered a couple of e-mails before opening a web browser and pulling up the federal immigration's website. She'd searched for a FAQ page but found nothing. It looked like she could start the process immediately by clicking on the big red button. She moved the mouse so the little arrow hovered over the box. She hesitated on depressing the left button on the mouse to start the process.

It seemed too easy.

She wanted to find a step-by-step instruction page, like a flowchart. She opened up another tab and Googled "How to get a green card through marriage". A ton of references came up on the screen, many of them from law firms. Perhaps that's what they should do, get a lawyer to do most of the hard work for them. She clicked on a random link and started to read.

The more she read, the more a ball of dread grew inside her.

Oh shit. No, this couldn't be possible. But it was. Written right there in black and white, damning their decision with every word she read.

What the hell was Gage going to say when she told him what she'd found out?

What the hell were they going to do?

What the hell had she been thinking, agreeing to this marriage?

• • •

"You're quiet—is everything okay?"

She and Gage were eating Chinese takeout at his kitchen table. All of her things were stored in a spare room. When Gage had opened the door to his penthouse condo, it hit Charlotte pretty quickly—just how wealthy her husband was. Oil had treated him well. The penthouse took up the whole floor of the building, more like a small house than an apartment. There were four bedrooms and five bathrooms, with each room decorated in tasteful colors and complementary accessories. Except it didn't look lived in. It had no soul. There were three pictures on the mantle above the fireplace in the living room—high school graduation pictures, from the quick glance she'd given them when Gage showed her around.

"Red?" Gage's hand landed on hers. "Is everything okay?"

"Yeah, sorry, just thinking about work and other stuff."

"Is there a problem at work? I forgot to ask what they said when you told them you and I were married and now you could get a green card."

"Well, Allen congratulated me about the wedding, but he was concerned about the fact that the person I'd married is a client of ours."

"I don't see how that would be a problem in our project dealings."

"Gage, you give me a hard time with just about everything I suggest your company does to protect the environment, to ensure that the land can be reused when you're done ripping the oil out. You make my job crazy some days."

"Hey, I have my own business to run and employees to look out for. Their livelihood depends on me and the decisions I make. But how about this: I'll consider your suggestions without being a bonehead about them from now on."

"It doesn't matter, because there won't be a next time."

"Are you saying they fired you? They can't fire you because you married me. Tell me exactly what happened."

"Stop, Gage. I didn't get fired. What's happened is, they've assigned your files to another person and now I've got his clients. I understand where the company is coming from, though. To be honest, with everything else going on in our lives, my working so closely with you on your rigs is probably not the best idea."

"I guess that's not so bad. What did they say when you told them about getting a green card?"

"I didn't say anything. I just said I'll being applying to stay in the States on a permanent basis. I didn't really want to say, 'Oh, hey, I'm married now and can get a green card.' You know what everyone is going to think."

"What?"

Charlotte rolled her eyes. Was he really so vague as to not get what she was hinting at? "The only reason we got married was so that I could become a permanent resident of the US. And even though that's the truth, it's really not a good idea to blab that out to everyone."

"I suppose, but what difference does it make why we got married? It's no one's business but ours. Our lives are the ones affected by the marriage. Not your bosses."

"It's the business of the Immigration Department, though. I did some reading up online about what we have to do to get my permanent residency. They really scrutinize applications that are marriage-based. Seems they've found that a lot of the marriages are shams—done just to get a green card."

"Wonder how long it took them to figure that one out," Gage said. "What steps do we have to take to prove that we aren't doing exactly what we're really doing?"

"This is wrong." She got up and started pacing around the kitchen. "This is all wrong!" she blurted out. "We shouldn't be doing this. I don't want to be deported or sent to jail for fraud. We shouldn't have gotten married. We can just get an annulment and everything will be okay. I'll go back to Australia, and when the year is up I'll sell you the land. You can do whatever you want with it. Yes, that's a good pl—"

Arms landed around her and her words were swallowed as Gage kissed her. His lips sipped at hers while his hands rubbed up and down her back in a soothing motion. She moaned as his teeth nipped at her bottom lip, encouraging her to open up for him. She couldn't deny him because, with his kiss, she was forgetting everything that swirled around in her mind: the mess they'd landed themselves into and how they were going to get out of it. All she could think about was feeling his bare skin beneath her hands.

She tugged at his shirt, releasing it from his pants. Finally, she could touch him. His skin was smooth and hot beneath her fingertips. She moved a little closer to him, feeling the evidence of his desire for her.

"I want you, Charlotte. How can you say this is wrong?"

His words were like a bucket of cold water on her, and she pulled her mouth away from his. How had she almost lost her mind again?

"What am I thinking? We really shouldn't be doing this, Gage."

Everything overwhelmed her, and she needed space. Without saying another word, she turned and walked out of the room. She needed to think.

Chapter 13

Gage, aroused and confused, watched Charlotte's retreating back. There appeared to be something more going on than her not working with his company anymore. It looked like she was having regrets about the marriage.

Hell, he'd had a couple of moments that day when he'd seen the ring on his finger and he'd asked himself whether he'd lost his mind. But then he remembered the end prize, and he believed the end justified the means. He'd also expected her to come home bursting with news on how to go about getting her green card.

He took a seat on the couch in the living room. Immediately, Oil Slick jumped up on his lap and did a couple of circles before curling up and settling in. He rubbed her soft fur, surprised at how quickly he'd come to enjoy the cat's company—not something he'd share just yet with Gavin.

"So, what do you think is up with Charlotte, Oil Slick? Should I go see what's wrong, or should I give her some space?"

The cat looked up at him with what looked like a *Duh, of course you need to go talk to her* look on her face.

He shook his head. If Gavin or Grayson could see him now, they'd think he'd lost his mind. But Oil Slick did have a point. He needed to talk to Charlotte to get to the bottom of the issues going on within her.

He set the cat down on the couch and made his way toward the room Charlotte had taken for her own. He had wanted to suggest she share the master suite with him, but he didn't think she'd like the idea, regardless of the fact that he'd seen the desire burning in her eyes on their wedding night. He knew she wanted him as much as he wanted her. Just like she'd wanted him not ten minutes ago.

He knocked on the door. "Charlotte, can I come in?"

"I want to be alone right now, Gage."

He rested his head on the wooden door frame. Any sane man would walk away and leave her to her thoughts. That was what she wanted, after all.

To hell with it. This wouldn't be his first insane decision. Throwing caution to the wind, he opened the door.

Charlotte sat in the middle of the bed, an open suitcase lying next to her. Gage didn't know if she was packing or unpacking her things.

"I thought I told you I wanted to be alone."

He walked over and sat down next to her, not touching her but close enough that he could if he wanted to. "I know, Red. But as you should know by now, I'm not that good at following instructions."

He was pleased to see his comment brought out a smile on her face.

"This is true."

The next instant a flash of black landed on the bed next to him. Oil Slick proceeded to walk across his legs until she was close enough to head-butt Charlotte for a pat.

He went to pick the cat up, but a hand halted his action.

"It's fine. I don't mind."

He nodded and left the cat where it was. The silence stretched between them. He wanted to come right out and ask her about her visa, since it was a good bet that was the issue with Charlotte's restlessness that evening. Instead, he let the quiet drag on until he couldn't stand it anymore.

"Talk to me, Charlotte. Tell me what's bothering you. A problem shared is a problem halved, as Dad would say."

"Did you ever imagine yourself getting married?"

The question threw him. It was the last thing he expected to hear from her, but it highlighted his suspicion that she was having second thoughts about what they'd done over the weekend.

He needed to word his response carefully. "I thought one day I would get married. Even have kids."

"But I'm guessing marrying someone so they could just get their permanent residency wasn't really one of the ways of doing it."

"It may not have been how I expected it to happen, but we're married now. There's no point in complaining about it. And don't forget, I get something out of it, as well."

"Maybe."

Gage's frustration level was growing higher with every passing second. Charlotte had never been wishy-washy in their dealings on a work level. She hadn't even been wishy-washy last night or on their wedding night, when she'd flat-out told him she wanted some space to herself. So why now?

"For God's sake, don't go all soap-opera dramatic on me again. Give it to me straight."

"Fine, don't say I didn't warn you." She took a deep breath while continuing to stroke Oil Slick, whose purring was a clear indication she was one happy cat. At least someone was. "It looks like I may be able to get a temporary green card."

"That's great. Why were you so worried about telling me that? It's good news, isn't it?"

"Sort of. After two years of marriage, I can then apply to replace the temporary one with a permanent card."

"So what's the big deal? Instead of being married for one year and then splitting up, we stay married another year and you get your card. Once it's all sorted out, then we can split up."

"Did you hear what I said, Gage? We have to be married for two years, not just one."

Okay, so maybe that might not have been what they'd planned on, but it didn't really matter to him.

"One year, two years. It's all relative. We'll be busy that second year with the land. Still doesn't sound too difficult to me."

"You'd think it would be that easy, wouldn't you? Stay married for two years instead of one. But it's not that simple, Gage. Our marriage is going to be scrutinized to ensure it's not fake. That it's not a marriage of convenience just to get a green card. But it is. That's exactly what our marriage is. We are essentially committing fraud. If the Immigration Department finds out that we are lying, I'll probably never be allowed back into the States again. And I've no idea what will happen to you. You may have to go to jail. I'm not sure that's a risk I want to take—with you or me. We should get our marriage annulled like I said earlier. It will be easier for both of us."

He sat quietly, trying to process all the information Charlotte had just dumped into his lap. Ever since she'd mentioned that marriage reality show, he'd thought that marrying her would be the perfect way to solve Charlotte's problem. And also get what he wanted—access to the land in twelve months' time or earlier if he could somehow convince Charlotte to change her stance. Plus, the immigration website had made it seem so easy. Huh. Did the people on the show that started them on this journey have to go through the same process she'd just mentioned? Or was the TV show sufficient for the immigration department to believe the marriages were real?

His dislike of research was coming back to bite him in the ass.

He twisted the wedding ring on his finger. His assistant knew about his marriage because she'd helped him with the flight arrangements and other necessary details. But he hadn't even told his brothers yet. Did he want to remove the ring? Admit he'd made yet another mistake?

No.

Marrying Charlotte wasn't a mistake. He wouldn't let it be a mistake.

"I take it by your silence you're seriously considering my suggestion of an annulment."

He transferred his gaze from his wedding ring to Charlotte. Her eyes, normally vibrant with life and laughter, were dull and sad, and he hated to see them that way.

Gage reached out and ran a finger down her soft cheek. "No." He leaned closer to her. "No, I'm not considering it. I don't want an annulment. I need to stay married to you, Charlotte Cooper. We'll sort everything out, and we'll convince everyone around us that we are in love and that our marriage is real. Including the federal immigration people."

He closed the distance between them and kissed her once again. He cupped the back of her neck, holding her close to him as he caressed her lips, his body igniting with fire for her once again. It seemed he only had to touch her and he wanted her. He could think of nothing better than spending each night with Charlotte in his arms. Waking her up each morning with a kiss on the neck. Traveling together to work. Hell, they could even discuss the state of the industry and how best to protect the environment while still achieving his oil-pumping goals before hell froze over.

"Ouch," she mumbled against his lips.

Charlotte broke the contact between them as she jumped up. "Dammit, Oil Slick, get your claws out of me."

The cat leaped to the ground and stalked out of the room with its tail swishing from side to side in annoyance. Gage laughed. "I swear, that cat is an old enemy of mine who has been sent back to torment me."

"You have a lot of enemies? Do I need to be worried?"

Her comment boosted his confidence. She was going to stick with their plan.

"Nope, you don't have to be worried."

"Good to know."

He reached out and took hold of her hand again. "So, are we good, Red? We'll stick with our plan?"

"Umm, maybe," she murmured before glancing back to the bed where, if his annoying feline hadn't interrupted them, they could've been on the way to making love right this moment. Gage's cock hardened even more at the thought and ached to be released.

He ran a hand through his hair, thinking a cold shower was a necessity right at that moment. "I'll leave you to unpack. But before I go, I want to say one more thing."

"What's that?"

"Nothing changes. Understand? I made you a promise to help you get your green card, and I won't go back on that."

"Thank you."

He nodded and walked out the door. At the end of the day, he was the winner. Not only did he have a beautiful wife, but now he had also access to an oil-rich piece of land. And considering the terms of their marriage were changing with regard to the length of time they stayed together, he could make a little amendment, too. He would adjust his own plans. Instead of waiting until after the marriage ended to get the land surveyed to find out how much oil was there, he would see if he could arrange it within the next couple of weeks. He'd already given the surveyor some preliminary information, which the surveyor had confirmed receipt of just before they'd left for Vegas. He'd just tell him to proceed with it now. It would be noninvasive, and Charlotte would never have to know.

Chapter 14

It was Saturday morning, and Charlotte had been a married woman for one week. She still slept by herself, and at the moment she and Gage were more roommates than husband and wife.

They hadn't talked anymore about her obtaining a green card or the process they would have to go through. She had found the name of a good immigration lawyer, but there was no way she was planning on contacting him until she was confident that she and Gage could present a united front and give the lawyer no doubts that they loved each other.

Her stomach plummeted at the thought of trying to fake being in love with Gage—not because she found him repulsive. It was just the opposite. The problem was, it would be easy to fall for Gage. He'd been nothing but the ultimate gentleman. He was being attentive and sweet, making sure she had everything she needed. And at the end of each night, he would give her a kiss on the forehead and head to his room.

His actions confused her.

"Hey, you want to take a drive?"

She yelped in fright. "My goodness, Gage, you could've at least knocked." She hadn't expected Gage to be up at almost eight in the morning. She figured he'd be one who slept in on the weekend. "I could've been changing or coming out of the bathroom in a towel."

Gage walked into her room, a first since the night she'd had her meltdown about the visa and the situation they now found themselves in. "Sorry. I'll remember next time. But, if you need help changing or drying off I'll be more than willing to help."

"Umm tempting as you may think that might be, not going to happen. So what do you want?"

"I thought we could spend the weekend down at Sweet Ridge. I haven't spoken to Gavin or Grayson since we got married. I figured it would be best if we told them our news face-to-face and together. You know, present a united front."

He hadn't spoken to his brothers about their marriage? She hadn't thought to ask him about it even though they'd Skyped her parents the other night and informed them. The initial surprise and worried looks on her parents' faces had concerned her. If they couldn't convince her parents, the people who knew her the best, they were in love and happy, how could they convince the immigration department? She needn't have worried. Gage had been super-attentive, and she hoped his actions and her reactions to him had been enough to convince her parents they had a genuine relationship. It had taken everything in her not to jump every time he touched her during their call. And it wasn't because she didn't like his touch. She found that at times, she wanted more little brushes against her arm or his arm around her waist. She'd lost count of the number of times she'd told herself it was a business arrangement, nothing else. The fact that her parents hadn't e-mailed her at all since the call confirmed to her that they'd convinced them all was well in their marriage. But could they fool Gavin and Grayson and the good folk of Sweet Ridge?

She studied Gage as he stood leaning against the chest of drawers. He looked relaxed, but she could see the slight tension in his shoulders, as if he expected her to turn him down. After everything he'd done for her, it wasn't too much to ask her to do this one thing for him.

"That sounds like fun. Where are we going to stay?"

"That's the best part. I thought we'd stay at the house on the land. What do you think?"

"I love that idea. But we'll need to get some sleeping bags and air mattresses. From memory I don't think there are any beds there." Charlotte couldn't contain her excitement at the idea of spending time in the house. Although knowing that she wouldn't be able to follow through with her plans of making it a holiday house dimmed the glow a little. But what did it matter? For the next few months, at least, they could make regular visits and she could clean the place up. Give it a fresh coat of paint on the inside and outside. She could always hope that when the survey had been completed in a year's time, it would show there wasn't a lot of oil on the property and then Gage wouldn't drill there after all.

"By the time we get packed and sorted out, we'll be able to stop at a camping store and pick up the necessary things. Can you recall whether there was a refrigerator in the kitchen?"

"I can't remember. But if there's not, we should be able to pick up a small one from Walmart that will serve us for the time being."

"That works. How long will it take you to pack a bag?"

"I can be done in thirty minutes."

"That will give me time to sort out what we have to take for Oil Slick."

"We're taking the cat?"

Gage looked at her as if she had three heads and each head asked an even sillier question than the previous one. "Of course. You don't think I'd leave her here on her own, do you? I've already had to replace three cushions on the couch before I started taking her to the office with me. I'm not going to leave her alone for a whole weekend. We'd come back to a wrecked house."

Charlotte laughed. "Wait till I tell your brothers a ball of fur has got you wrapped around her tail."

Gage shrugged it off with a smile. "Eh, they've teased me for worse things. And Gavin's dog, Merle, goes everywhere with him, so he won't blink an eye at me taking the cat with me wherever I go. He was the one who gave me the leash when I became Oil Slick's new daddy."

"What about packing for yourself? I see you didn't mention that. I hope you don't plan on spending the whole weekend in the same clothes."

Gage chuckled. "I've already packed."

"Oh, you were that sure I was going to say yes and go with you, were you?"

"Of course I was. I knew you wouldn't need much encouragement to go see the house. I'll see you in thirty."

He breezed out of the room, leaving her standing there, wondering if she'd just been conned.

• • •

The drive down to Sweet Ridge passed without too much drama. Charlotte fully expected to travel down in two cars, as she knew not everything they were taking and needed to buy would fit in Gage's sports car or her sedan. So she was taken aback at the shiny blue SUV idling under the building's portico. It seemed Gage had two cars. Once everything was packed in and Oil Slick fastened into the special seat Gage had purchased, they started their trip, only stopping at Gander Mountain, where Gage went in and purchased everything they needed. She stayed in the SUV with Oil Slick. While waiting, she let herself dream of future trips like this … only instead of having the cat in the car, there were two children chatting happily in the back.

She yanked herself out of the daydream pretty quickly. No matter what her imagination might think she wanted, her practical side had enough sense not to get too carried away with fanciful thoughts of a future with Gage.

Their marriage was temporary—if you could call having to be married for two years "temporary". Splitting after two years would give everyone the impression they'd given it a red-hot go.

They pulled up at the house. After not seeing it for a couple of weeks, she'd forgotten how cute it looked and how much it fit in, sitting on the rise in the land.

"Why don't you go inside and start opening the windows to let some fresh air in while I unpack? I told Gavin and Grayson we'd meet them at the Silver Spurs at one."

"Do they know I'm coming with you?"

Gage leaned over and kissed her quickly on the cheek. The action was unexpected. "Nope. I thought I'd surprise them."

Oh boy, were they going to be surprised. "Are you planning on telling them the real reason we got married?"

Gage pulled a couple of bags out of the back of the SUV. "Nah, I've been doing some research of my own after our conversation, and in case we do get investigated, it would be best we keep things about our arrangement on the down-low. The fewer people who know, the better."

"That makes sense," she said as she walked away toward the house. She opened the door. The musty odor of abandonment assailed her nostrils—what she'd expected the house to smell like the first time she'd visited. She should probably ask around town to find out who had looked after it before and get them to continue to do so.

As she walked around the house, methodically opening all the windows, she let herself think about Gage's suggestion about presenting their marriage.

He was all Mr. Executive this weekend, treating their marriage like the business deal it was. And he was good at business deals. He'd started out in menial jobs on rigs before ascending to the executive suite. According to the magazine articles she'd read about him, he had a natural instinct for the oil business.

She should probably get those details about his journey up the oil rig ranks if they were going to pull off this marriage charade.

But that would be later—and especially not in front of his family.

Charlotte had just finished opening all the windows upstairs when Gage appeared on the landing.

"Do you want your bag in the master bedroom, seeing as this is your house and all?" he joked…maybe.

"Sure, that sounds as it should be. I haven't checked to see if we have running water, have you?"

"Nope, but I know this house is connected to the town water supply, as well as having a rainwater tank at the back. I'll check to see if things are working."

She nodded, even though he had already walked away. She headed back downstairs while a million other thoughts about the house entered her mind. The living room would need a good cleaning, even though it had been reasonably dust-free the last time they were there. The soft tread of shoes hitting the hardwood floors sounded behind her. She turned as Gage joined her in the room.

"Did you check to see if we have a fridge?" she asked.

"Yeah, I turned it on, but it needs a clean-out."

"Maybe after lunch we can stop off and get some cleaning supplies. I should've thought of that before we left Houston."

"We should make a list of everything we need and what needs a quick fix. This house hasn't been lived in for a long time. I'm surprised it's not covered in more layers of dust than it already is."

"Yeah, I'm thinking it was cleaned regularly until the first trip I made down here. I wonder if Rodney told whoever was cleaning the place to stop. I may call him on Monday to find out and get them to go back to a regular schedule. I'll ask around town as well."

"Sounds like a plan. I mean, even if we come down each weekend, I don't want to spend all of our time cleaning the place."

Come down every weekend? Why would Gage want to do that when he hadn't wanted to before? She added that to her mental list of things to ask him about later.

"True," she murmured.

Gage pulled his phone out of his pocket and started making some notes on it. Well, she assumed they were notes. He looked up and saw her watching him.

"What? Is something wrong?"

She shook her head. "No, it's just that this whole thing"—she waved her arm around the room—"is so very domesticated."

Gage put his phone in his pocket and walked toward her. When he got within touching distance she held her breath. Disappointment laced through her when he crossed his arms across his chest instead of what she'd anticipated he'd do: take her into his arms. "And that is wrong, because…?"

"It's not wrong, just unexpected."

"Right."

"Anyway, we need that list made before we have to go into town and meet your brothers for lunch."

"Ahh, yes, lunch with my dear brothers. It will be fine, you know."

"I wasn't too worried, but do you think we should get our stories straight about our *relationship*? When I first them we hardly acted like we were in love then, and on the brink of marriage."

"Don't worry, Red. Trust me."

Trust him?

Yeah. Right. Okay.

She didn't know how Gage could be so relaxed and flippant, but they were his brothers and she couldn't come up with a better idea, so she'd just go along with exactly what he asked. If they were about to meet her own brothers, she'd be panicking. Being the youngest—and a girl—her brothers had always taken their big-brother roles seriously, giving any guys who called around to see her a hard time. Of course, living in other countries as they grew up had made her siblings extra-vigilant in their duties to make sure she was safe. At the time she had hated them for embarrassing her. Now she wished they were here to do their protective routine. Not that she needed protecting from Gage, but having Sam, Greg, and Brad close by would've been nice.

"Fine. I'll sit and smile and nod then, shall I?"

"That's the worst possible thing you could do. After the way you basically told them to back off from asking any questions about the land the last time we were here, if you're meek and mild, they'll definitely know something is up."

"Right." She looked at her watch and saw that it was nearly time to head into town. "Well, if we're going to do this, we need to leave in the next ten minutes."

"Okay, let me take a quick look around to see what might need a repair. The sleeping bags are in a safe place so Oil Slick can't get to them. And the water is running in the bathrooms so you can use one if you need to."

Charlotte shuddered at the thought. "I'm not touching any of the bathrooms until I've had a chance to clean them."

Gage laughed. "Are you a prissy princess, Red?"

"No. I've lived in some pretty interesting places, but because we lived in the ex-pat compounds, everything was always clean at least. This house hasn't been lived in in I don't know how many years. And even though it was regularly cleaned before, it hasn't been since our last visit. So, yes, when it comes to using the facilities, I want to make sure I'm not going to get any nasty surprises, thank you very much."

"Uh-huh, as I said, prissy."

She rolled her eyes and then cocked her head. "Is that Oil Slick I hear tearing at something?"

Gage's demeanor changed in a flash, and he was off to the living room before she could say "*just joking*". That would teach him for being a smart-ass with her. As she looked around the kitchen, she couldn't help but wish the easy camaraderie they were sharing now would continue.

But since she was about to face his brothers, she knew it wouldn't.

Chapter 15

Gage tightened his hold on Charlotte's hand as they approached the Silver Spurs, the rings he'd given her digging into his fingers. He hadn't wanted to let on back at the house, but he was as nervous and apprehensive about this meeting with his brothers as she was.

He knew Gavin and Grayson were already at the bar. He'd seen their cars in the parking lot.

Tension had intensified Charlotte's features, making her look like she was about to face a firing squad. He stopped and pulled her against him.

"What?" she asked.

He didn't say anything, just smoothed her hair back from her face before lowering his head and kissing her. Her arms wound around his neck and she aligned her body with his. He wanted to forget about meeting his brothers. His body had being dying to sample her again, to find out what made her sigh, what made her moan, what made her scream in pleasure. He wanted to know it all, but he still sensed her apprehension in taking that final step.

Reluctantly, he pulled back, breaking their embrace. Her face now held a dreamy, more relaxed expression. Her lips were plump from his kiss. He liked the look on her. His cock strained against his jeans, wanting to be released from the confines of the fabric. He hoped his hard-on wouldn't be too obvious when he sat down at the table.

"If we'd walked in a few minutes ago, they would've known something wasn't right. Now you have the look of a newly married woman," he commented as he led her up the stairs to the bar.

Charlotte looked down at his jeans, and he couldn't stop his flesh from twitching in excitement. "While you look like you're in pain."

He laughed, letting her enter the bar before him. As she passed he whispered in her ear, "Maybe you can ease my pain later on."

She whipped her head around to look at him, the strands of her red hair catching the sunlight streaming through the front door. *Sweet Texas fire.*

"Maybe," she responded with a wink.

"Gage. Over here." Gavin's voice reached him, and he lifted his hand in acknowledgment and headed in their direction. Speculation entered his brothers' eyes when they saw who he was holding on to. It was almost comical the way both of his brothers' eyebrows rose so high on their faces. Macy, on the other hand, had a huge, knowing smile on her face, as if she'd predicted this would happen.

They got to the table, and after Gage held out a chair for Charlotte, he took the one next her. He noticed Charlotte kept her hands under the table so he placed his left hand on her right thigh.

For a few seconds no one said anything, even though he knew his brothers were champing at the bit to ask what he was doing in town again, why was he in Sweet Ridge with Charlotte, and more importantly, why he'd been holding Charlotte's hand.

"Y'all got married, didn't you?" Macy blurted out.

Gavin choked on the beer he'd just taken a sip of, and Grayson burst out laughing.

"Baby, how many beers have you had to make you say that?" Gavin asked as he wiped his chin.

"I haven't even finished my first, as you well know. How you boys could've missed the rock on Charlotte's finger and the shiny gold ring on Gage's when they walked through the door is beyond me." Macy cocked her head. "Besides, they haven't said anything to deny it, have they?"

Three pairs of eyes landed on him and Charlotte. The tension he'd so effortlessly kissed out of her a few minutes ago returned full-force if the way her leg felt like a bar of steel under his fingers was any indication.

Grayson was the first to break the death stare going on around the table. “Dude, is Macy right? Are you guys married?”

Gage removed his hand from Charlotte’s leg, and with slow, deliberate movements he curled his arm around her shoulder, letting his hand hang down, the gold ring on his finger on display for all to see.

“Shut the fu—” Macy’s hand slapped over Gavin’s mouth to stop the expletive.

“Seriously, Gavin? What’s the big deal?” Gage tried for nonchalance, but he wasn’t sure he succeeded.

“What have you done?” Grayson asked. “I thought you’d outgrown your impulsive tendencies. This is madness. What are you thinking?”

Grayson’s words hurt. Gage suspected his family wouldn’t be happy with the news, but he hadn’t expected them to be so rude about it. Nor for Grayson to bring up his impulsive past.

“You know, I don’t appreciate the way you’re talking about my husband. Neither of us is mad or insane. And Gage was neither impulsive nor reckless when he asked me to marry him. And neither was I when I said yes.” Charlotte turned to him, and he could see the fire of anger in her eyes. But there was something else there, too: a fierceness to protect and defend him.

Was this even real? If not, she was pulling out all the stops to act the loving wife. She leaned toward him and smiled. He could feel his face stretching into his own smile. Her eyes never left his as she continued. “He went out of his way to create the most wonderful wedding for me. It was more than any girl could ask for.”

Yep, she was acting, and … well, he might as well take center stage with her.

Not caring that his brothers and Macy and no doubt everyone else in the Silver Spurs was watching, Gage hooked a finger under her chin. "Thank you, Red," he whispered before once again tasting those sweet lips. While he wanted to make the kiss last, he still had enough awareness to realize they weren't alone.

As he broke the connection between them, he couldn't help but smile at Charlotte's little groan of disappointment. For the first time in his life, he had a taste of what it was like to have someone who supported him—who was willing to go out on a limb and stand by his side. It felt damn good, even if it was a pretense.

"Well, if these two aren't in love, my name isn't Macy Young." Macy leaned forward with a big grin on her face. "Unlike these two buffoons here, I'm very happy for you both. I want to hear all the details about y'alls' wedding. *And* I want to know why we weren't invited."

As a tension breaker, it worked. But he could still see the skepticism in both Gavin and Grayson's eyes—and Gage knew the moment he was alone with them, his brothers were going to pounce on him and ask him if he'd married Charlotte just to get his hands on the land. While it was technically true, he had to make sure they didn't know that. He needed to make sure he had his answers straight before answering the questions he knew they were going to fire at him.

"Where did you tie the knot?" Gavin asked.

"Vegas," Charlotte answered. "In a cute little chapel Gage picked out."

"Oh, please tell me y'all didn't get married by an Elvis impersonator?" Macy asked.

Gage laughed as he threaded his fingers through Charlotte's and placed their joined hands on the table. "No, we didn't. It was a respectable chapel, and the man who led the proceedings was very sweet, wasn't he, Red?"

"Yes, and his wife was lovely, too. She took photos of the ceremony and afterward. We should be getting those pictures soon."

"Where did you go for your wedding dinner? Was it somewhere nice? And seriously, girl, you gotta show me your ring up close." Macy got up out of her seat. "Baby, you need to move so I can sit next to Charlotte. We have a lot to talk about."

Gage couldn't help but smile at Macy's enthusiasm; he caught her eye as she took over Gavin's seat. He mouthed a "*thank you*" to her. She nodded in response. At least there was one person who supported him and Charlotte. He also had a feeling Gavin was going to get a serious talking-to when they got home.

Gage sat back, his fingers caressing the back of Charlotte's neck as she showed Macy her rings and Macy ooohhed and ahhhed over them.

He deliberately didn't catch his brothers' eyes. They could wait. He was enjoying being out with his wife, a feeling he could easily get used to.

• • •

Gage pushed his plate away. After the initial discomfort from their announcement, the tension around the table had settled down and they'd all enjoyed what was now a celebratory belated-wedding lunch.

"I'm just going to the bathroom with Macy," Charlotte whispered in his ear before giving him a quick kiss on the cheek. No doubt for the benefit of his brothers, but he wasn't going to complain.

"Okay."

He watched the two women as they walked toward the bathroom, mentally counting *one, two, three, f—*

"You married her for the land, didn't you?" Grayson demanded. He should've known Grayson would be the one to fire off the first question. He'd always taken his big-brother role seriously.

"It was a consideration we discussed when we decided to marry."

"You run a multimillion-dollar company—did you even think about a prenup?" Grayson was clearly fired up by the whole situation. "What happens if this marriage doesn't work out? You could end up with nothing—not the land *nor* the company you worked so hard to build."

Touché. The odds that Charlotte would turn out to be a bitch and take him to the cleaners seemed small now, but…

"Shit, Gage, I can see from your face you didn't even consider that scenario. I can't believe you didn't do all you needed to do to protect your company. I really thought the days of you making stupid mistakes like this were over." Grayson shook his head in disbelief.

That was enough. "Shut up, Grayson. Marrying Charlotte is not a mistake. And you know what? Maybe I'll take my twenty-five percent of Guac Olé and align myself with Becca come September first. And perhaps our first order of business will be to replace the current CEO. What do you think of that business decision?"

Gage saw the anger rising in Grayson's face and the look of shock on Gavin's. In reality, Gage would never betray his brother like that, but he needed to get Grayson to back off.

"You wouldn't dare," Grayson said. "You know Guac Olé is my life."

"Yeah, I do, Gray. I know you bleed guacamole, but I don't need you to run my life. I'm thirty, for fuck's sake. Just drop it. The relationship between Charlotte and me is complicated. Quite frankly, I don't care what either of you think of my marriage. It's my life, and I'm not making a mistake. So both of you need to listen and understand one thing." He leaned forward so his brothers could appreciate the importance of what he was about to say next. "Charlotte is my wife. I expect you to respect her. The circumstances of our marriage are none of your business. Just know that when you attack, condemn, or are rude to Charlotte, you're doing all those things to me. Remember, I've walked away before. I can do it again."

He sat back in his chair, confident he'd gotten his message across. Damn, he really should've tried harder in drama class.

The girls returned to their seats, and he immediately reached for Charlotte's hand and brought it to his lips.

"You okay?" she asked.

"I am now," he responded, and he was. Having Charlotte beside him made him happy, if only because in this situation he knew she was more friend than foe.

"Is everything okay between you and your brothers?"

Gage looked over to where his brothers sat. Gavin was, like him and Charlotte, having his own quiet conversation with Macy. From the look on Macy's face, Gavin wasn't asking her whether she enjoyed her meal—they were sharing things that couples in love do. When Macy leaned over and kissed him, it confirmed everything he thought. Grayson, on the other hand, was having a love affair with his phone. The guy needed to chill.

"It will be," he said.

"I don't want to be the cause of tension between you and your brothers. Family is important."

He kissed her hair. "It'll be fine. Don't worry." He finished off his drink. "You ready to go?"

"I am if you are."

They stood together. "Well, this has been fun," Gage started. "But we've got to go get some things for the house."

Gavin came around and hugged Charlotte, a gesture Gage appreciated. Then Gavin turned and hugged him, as well. "You look happy, Gage, and that's all I want."

"Thanks, bro. That means a lot."

"Oh, how's the cat?"

Gage rolled his eyes. "You do realize that cat is a demon."

Gavin laughed. "She was feisty at the surgery for sure."

"Are you talking about Oil Slick?" Charlotte piped in.

"Oil Slick? He tossed around the idea of changing her name from Lady Marceline to Oil Slick when he came to the surgery. I never thought he would stick with it."

Charlotte leaned into his side. "It suits the cat well, and no matter what he may or may not have said, Gage enjoys having her around. You do know he takes little Oil Slick to work, right?"

Gage couldn't stop the flush from growing up his neck. He knew it was happening because Gavin was laughing his head off.

When he stopped laughing, he said, "You take the cat to work? Oh, little brother, that is classic."

"If I didn't, she'd be wrecking my whole damn house. I need to send you a bill for the replacement cushions I had to get because of that damn cat."

"Sorry, bro, anything that happens after the animals leave my clinic is the responsibility of the pet owner. If you send me a bill, I'll just send it back."

Gage clutched at his chest. "I'm wounded."

"You're full of shit, Gage," Gavin retorted.

Gage slapped Gavin on the back. Grayson stood to the side, watching the exchange. Gage walked over to him.

"Are we good?" he asked Grayson.

"As long as you don't do what you threatened to do, then yeah, we're good."

"I may be a jerk of a brother sometimes, but I wouldn't deliberately hurt you. But you need to understand I won't have you bad-mouthing Charlotte."

Gage straightened his spine under Grayson's intense look. After a few seconds Grayson nodded. "Hell, even I acknowledge you've created a successful business. And I have to believe after what you've been through, you know what you're doing."

"Yeah, you do."

"Then congratulations on your marriage, bro." Grayson slapped him on the back. They were back on even ground, thank God.

"So, Cowboy, you ready to go? That house isn't going to get cleaned by itself," Charlotte interjected.

"Yep."

Gage slung his arm around his wife and gave his brothers one last wave. "Drop by the land Charlotte inherited tomorrow at lunchtime. We'll grill some burgers."

Both Gavin and Grayson nodded.

As they walked out the door, Gage let himself relax. One hurdle cleared. Now if he could only find out where that damn key belonged.

Chapter 16

Charlotte wiped down the kitchen counter. It wasn't exactly shining, but it was clean and she would be happy to cut food on it. The house held the distinctive scent of bleach and furniture polish, and the staircase, windowsills, and mantels were all free of dust. After the last three hours she could safely say she'd be comfortable using any of the bathrooms in the house.

Gage had attended to a couple of minor repairs to some doors and the porches. Overall they'd had a productive afternoon.

But it had been a stressful lunch, and she'd worried that when she and Macy went to the restroom, they'd come back to find the boys fighting. She had seen the tension in Gage when they'd returned. He told her in the car that he and Grayson had words, but it wasn't anything she needed to worry about. The fact that Gage had invited everyone out for lunch proved the point. Still, she couldn't help but worry things were going to be uncomfortable again tomorrow.

The back door opened and Gage knocked his feet on the side of the door frame before coming in.

"How does everything look outside?" she asked.

"It doesn't look too bad. There doesn't seem to be any structural issues with the house. But I want to go up to the attic to see if there are any indications of leaks," he said as he walked over to the sink to wash his hands.

"I can't help but think you're going to find a problem with the roof."

"Why do you say that?"

She shrugged her shoulders. "I don't know. The house has been empty for so long. No one has lived in it, so you'd think there'd be some issues with it. But saying that, it's like Jack kept up the maintenance. I mean, sure, there was dust on things that first day I came here, but not as much as I expected."

"Maybe Dad did. He never said anything to me when we talked about the land just before he died."

"Except that you were going to inherit it," she drawled wryly.

"Yeah, that. I still don't understand why he changed his will."

"I've got no idea why Jack thought I should receive this piece of land."

"I know, and I haven't said it before and I probably should've. I'm sorry for what I said to you that day in your office. I shouldn't have suggested you and he had anything more than a friendship."

"Thank you. I appreciate it. And"—she looked at him with a wry grin—"we've kind of come a long way from there, haven't we?"

Gage laughed, the sound rich and deep. "That we have." He placed a quick kiss on her lips. "Now, I'm about to head to the attic, so if you don't hear from me in an hour, send a search party. You never know what might be lurking in the attic of an old house."

Charlotte shuddered as he walked away, hoping there was nothing creepy in the attic. She stood in the kitchen for a few minutes, and against her better judgment, her mind walked down the path to a future she'd closed off earlier in the day while she waited in the car at Gander Mountain. The one where she and Gage had, against all odds, fallen in love with each other. Where they came to this house on weekends and had Sunday lunches with his brothers and their significant others. Where they had a couple of children who completed their family. And where at night Gage would take her into his arms and make love to her.

It was a wonderful dream. Unfortunately, it was a future that wouldn't come to fruition. The scary thing was, it hadn't been too much of a hardship to play "happy wife" today. To look into his eyes and tell everyone that he'd created a magical wedding day for them.

Charlotte sighed. There were bedrooms that needed to be dusted and airbeds to make up. She was no Disney princess, and Gage was no Prince Charming.

• • •

She made her way downstairs, glancing at her watch as she went. It was almost dinnertime. She was glad they'd decided to buy a frozen pizza to have for dinner. The thought of having to prepare and cook something didn't hold a high appeal after spending the afternoon cleaning the house.

She expected to see Gage in the kitchen. She'd heard him moving around in the attic while she'd been working upstairs, but there hadn't been any sounds for the last half hour so she'd assumed he'd come back down.

"Gage?" she called out, his name echoing around the unfurnished rooms. They really needed to go get some chairs for everyone to sit on tomorrow, or it was going to be one massive picnic.

She headed outside—maybe he was working on something in the backyard. But she still couldn't find him.

The car still stood in the driveway, and she knew he wouldn't leave without telling her.

Starting to worry that something had happened to him, she made her way back into the house and methodically walked through all the rooms downstairs and then upstairs. There she found the access to the attic still down.

"Gage?" she called up into the opening. "Are you up there?"

"Yeah."

She waited to see if he would come down, but the area at the top of the access stairs remained black, like a gaping hole into nowhere.

She couldn't explain the feeling of apprehension that came over her when she placed her foot on the rickety wooden steps and made her way up into the dark cavern. The area was huge and lit only by a bare light bulb.

Her eyes adjusting to the dim light, she looked around and found Gage surrounded by some sheet-covered shapes and a couple of boxes.

"Are you okay?"

"I'm not sure, Red," came Gage's response.

"So, we have a leak and we have to replace the roof?"

"If only it were that simple. A replacement roof I could deal with better than this."

She squatted down next to him, putting her hand on his knee. "Talk to me, Gage. What's going on?"

He held a box out to her. "This."

She took the old wooden box the size of a large jewelry box. The shiny wood had two entwined hearts in a lighter-colored wood inlaid on the top. At each corner little flowers were etched in gold; the entire piece looked handmade. She lifted it closer and twisted it to get more light onto it. Beneath the flowers it appeared there were two initials entwined as the stems. She couldn't make out the letters though. She would need better light.

"It's beautiful. Do you know who it belongs to?"

"No."

Charlotte examined the box again and then glanced back at Gage, trying to process the reason for the despair emanating from him.

In the waning sunlight, the shadows lengthened, taking on eerie shapes. She couldn't stop the shudder of fear from rippling through her.

"Um, let's take this downstairs. Get a better look at it."

She made the move to stand, but noticed Gage hadn't moved. His reaction to the box seemed over the top.

"Gage, come on, let's go downstairs and maybe you can tell me why this box is freaking you out so much."

She wrapped her fingers around his upper arm and tugged. Finally, it seemed to break him out of his stupor.

"Sorry." He looked around as if only then noticing how dark the room had gotten. "Yeah, let's get out of here."

They made their way down the steps and into the living room. As they passed a light switch, Charlotte flicked it on. She needed light after the darkness of the attic. The fact that they were out in the middle of nowhere hadn't bothered her until that moment.

She jumped and let out a little cry of fright when Gage put his arm around her.

"Are you scared, Red?"

"Did you not see those creepy shadows in the attic? Yes, I'm scared. We're not exactly surrounded by civilization here, either, you know."

Gage laughed and pulled her close. The laughter was a welcome sound after the melancholy aura that had surrounded them in the attic.

"We're safe here, Charlotte. And there is nothing but sheet-covered furniture in the attic. I checked it thoroughly. Not even any indication of rats or other lovely creatures taking up residence under the roof."

"Well, I guess that's reassuring since I hadn't given any thoughts to rats living in my house until now."

They entered the kitchen and Charlotte placed the box on the kitchen counter.

"You ready for our gourmet dinner?" she asked Gage as he opened the refrigerator.

"Pizza for two?" he asked.

"You chose it, so yes, pizza for two."

Charlotte spent the next few minutes turning on the oven and placing the pizza inside. She was aware of Gage moving over to look at the box. Out of the corner of her eye, she saw him make a move to touch it and then pull back.

"What is it about that box that has rattled you so much, Gage?"

"Rattled? What do you mean by that?"

"You almost seem afraid of it."

"Ah." He pushed a hand through his hair, making the ends stand up endearingly. "I wouldn't say I'm afraid of it, but it's clearly something that was a beloved memento to someone. I want to know why it's in the attic of a house on a piece of land my father owned for more than thirty years."

"Did it belong to your mother? I know she's passed. Jack told me, and, well, you haven't mentioned her."

Gage shook his head. "I don't think it's Mom's. I don't remember seeing it before, but she died when I was five. I don't remember too much about what she had. Maybe that's why it's here. Maybe it meant so much to Dad, he couldn't bear seeing it."

While that seemed like the most likely explanation, it still didn't explain why Gage was so transfixed that he could barely move when he discovered it in the attic.

"There's more to this than you're letting on. So how about you tell me."

"I'm not sure, but the shape of the keyhole on the lock looks as if the key Dad left me will fit in it."

"That's a good thing, isn't it?"

Gage turned back to the box and picked it up. As he examined the lock more closely, she watched his face, wanting to see if there was a flicker of emotion to indicate why he didn't want to associate with the box.

"I'm not sure it's a good thing at all."

And they called women frustrating. Gage was frustrating the hell out of her at the moment. "How can having a memory of your mother's be a bad thing? You want to know what the key belongs to, don't you?"

"Yes."

"Well, now you have a possible way of finding out, so I don't know why you're being such a pansy about it all. We will take it back home tomorrow, get the key, and then you can open it and put everything to rest."

"But what if I don't like what I find inside?"

"What are you expecting to find? The answer as to why your father left me this property? Unless he had someone place it here between him changing his will and his death, I don't think you're going to get the answers you need."

"Maybe. Maybe not. He left me a note as well with the key. Maybe the answer to the note will be in the box."

"What did the note say?"

"'*Son, the key to everything is happiness.*' So while I want to open the box, I'm also not sure I want to know that the key I hold is what's going to lead me to happiness."

The timer on the oven went off, giving her a few minutes to comprehend the riddle that was Gage's note. It was a wide and encompassing statement to say that the key to everything was happiness. Happiness came in many forms. She somehow doubted the contents of the box were a magic elixir to finding it.

She would say that contentment within oneself was the key to happiness.

Cutting the pizza into slices, she placed them on the paper plates they'd purchased and handed one to Gage while she picked up the other. He went to pick up the box again.

"Leave it, Gage. And while I know it's bugging you, you can't do anything about it until tomorrow. Maybe you can show Gavin and Grayson the box when they come for lunch. They might have a better memory of it sitting on your mother's dresser than you do, and that will solve one part of the mystery."

"Yeah, you're probably right."

They went into the living room and sat down on the camp chairs they'd purchased. They ate quietly. When Charlotte had finished, she cocked her ear.

"Is that rain?"

Gage got up and walked over to the window. "Yep, it is."

"I didn't notice any rain in the forecast."

"Do we really not have anything to say to each other except to talk about the weather? We're doomed."

"I don't think we're there yet. But I do think because I cooked, you should do the dishes."

Gage rolled his eyes. "But they're going to take me hours," he whined, teasing her with a wink. They both knew all he had to do was put the two paper plates in the trash can.

"It's only fair, you know."

"I suppose you expect me to start doing this when we get home, too."

She shrugged. "Guess we'll have to wait and see. Of course, if you want to get out of doing the dishes, all you have to do is cook."

His laughter echoed around the room as he collected the plates and wandered into the kitchen.

She stretched back in her chair. There was an old bathtub upstairs, and the temptation to take a long bath to soothe her tired muscles was strong. Only they hadn't picked up any bubble bath when they went shopping earlier in the day.

Charlotte looked at her watch. It wasn't too late, but she doubted that any of the shops stayed open until ten in the evening like the shops in Houston did. It had been easy to get used to shopping at any hour of the day, seven days a week, something that was just becoming more popular in Australia.

"What do you want to do for the rest of the evening?"

Without thinking she voiced her thoughts. "I would love to test out that bathtub in the master bathroom. Pity I don't have any bubble bath, though."

"I bought some shower gel. You can always put that in the water. It should create the bubbles you want. That is, if you don't mind smelling a bit like me."

The thought of smelling like Gage sent sensual darts of pleasure arrowing through her. She crossed her arms across her breasts as her nipples peaked against her bra.

"Sure." Her voice broke partway through the short word. She cleared her throat and tried again. "Sure, that would be great. I think I could handle smelling like you for one day."

"Stay right there. I'll fix everything up for you."

As Gage made his way upstairs, her earlier fantasies of a future together with Gage fired through her brain again. Only this time extinguishing the flames became a little more difficult.

Chapter 17

Gage rolled over and tried to get comfortable. Sleeping on an air mattress was luxury in comparison to some of the places he'd slept while working on the rigs.

Maybe it was knowing Charlotte was sleeping two doors down that was keeping him awake, even if it was no different from their sleeping arrangements for the past week at his condo.

Or it was more likely that he couldn't stop thinking about her being naked in the bathtub and now smelling like his shower gel. He'd spent that whole time trying to control the urge to go up and join her. The tub was plenty big enough for the both of them.

He groaned as his dick responded by jumping to life. He'd already taken one cold shower; he didn't need to be taking another one. He had to think of something to get his body under control. Jerking off was one option, but it would be just his luck if Charlotte walked in on him. Would she finish him off? His body liked that idea.

You could seduce her.

Oh fuck, like he needed any more advice from the voice that had gotten him in this mess in the first place. Although the idea had merit, but when and if he and Charlotte ever made love, it would be in his nice king-size bed in his master bedroom at the condo. Not on a camping store air mattress.

A creaking floorboard dismissed the thought of seducing Charlotte. He strained his ears a little to see if he could pick up the sound again, or if he'd imagined it.

Eeeeee.

Nope, he'd heard it again, and it was right outside his bedroom door.

"Gage?" Her voice whispered across the room.

He sat up. "Red? What's wrong?"

His eyes had adjusted to the darkness, and he could make out her silhouette as she stood in the doorway.

"I, um, well, I can't sleep."

"Welcome to the club," he muttered.

"What?"

"Nothing. Why can't you sleep?"

"Can I come in? I don't want to have this conversation standing in your doorway."

"Sure, come in and sit on the bed." He shifted over to one side to make room for her.

The mattress dipped when Charlotte sat down, and he had to grab at the side so as not to fall into her. He could make out the rigid line of her back. She looked like she was about to snap. He hesitated for a fraction of second before he placed his hand lightly on her back.

"Lie down, Red, and tell me what's going on."

Beneath his hand, he felt the breath *whoosh* out of her, and he bit back a groan as she lay down next to him. He rolled on his side so that he could spoon her from behind. She lay on top of the blankets while he lay beneath. He angled his hips away to prevent pressing his erection into her.

"It's so stupid, really," she started on a whisper.

"What's stupid?" He kept his voice low and modulated to encourage her to continue.

"I started thinking about the attic, and I know you said nothing was up there, but I kept imagining I could hear things moving about. And well, you know, old house, sitting in the middle of nowhere. It has 'horror movie' written all over it."

He couldn't help it; he burst out laughing. "I've stayed here before. You really are safe. I've got my gun. We'll be fine."

She pulled out of his embrace and rolled over to face him. "Why didn't you tell me you carried a gun? Did you have it on you today when we were at lunch?"

"Hey, slow down. It's Texas, pretty much everyone has a gun. I do have a conceal-and-carry permit, but it depends where I'm going as to whether I take it. I can assure you that whenever we've gone out I haven't carried my gun with me. I brought it down here, though, because, well, there could've been critters here that we might have needed to get rid of. I don't take carrying a gun lightly."

He could see her looking skeptically at him. He reached out to touch her face. "Red, I know you can look after yourself, but Jack Cooper taught his sons to look after their own. We're married now, so that includes me looking out for you. But I will tell you if I'm carrying or not. Is that okay?"

She nodded after a moment. "I'm still not used to the gun laws here. It's so different back in Australia."

"I know. Now roll over again, so I can hold you."

Gage knew he was playing with fire, but he couldn't deny that he liked holding Charlotte. He'd wanted her ever since their wedding night. The desire had only increased. Now, with her so close, smelling like both Charlotte and his shower gel, he wanted to forget about his promise to himself and take her now rather than in his bed. A certain part of his anatomy wished he'd do the same, too. He had to find some other way to divert his attention.

"Tell me something," he said.

"What?"

"That weekend when you came down and looked at the place, you told me you'd changed your mind about selling. Why?"

"It doesn't really matter what my reasons were then. Come twelve months' time, you'll own the land."

The sadness in her voice couldn't be denied, and he almost felt bad for going ahead and arranging the survey. But they had an agreement, and with the money she would receive from the royalties of the oil production from the property, she'd be able to buy ten properties just like this one or an even better one.

"Let's pretend that wasn't happening. Why this place? Why Sweet Ridge?"

Charlotte didn't say anything for the longest time, and he began to suspect she'd fallen asleep when she started speaking.

"This place would be my weekend house. It's not too far away from Houston to be able to come down here every weekend. The Gulf Coast isn't that far away, either, and while the beaches aren't fabulous here, it's still nice to be able to know that on a hot day I could drive a little way and take a walk on the beach."

"Seems a lot of work to keep up a place this big for just you."

"Well, I guess once we split up, I'll take some time out from getting into another relationship. But I do hope to one day fall in love and marry again. Maybe have some kids. Then it would be fun to come down here—put a swing set in the backyard so they can play. And who knows, if my husband and I like it down here, maybe we'd relocate so the kids could go to school in Sweet Ridge. You and your brothers turned out all right."

No matter how hard Gage tried to stop it, he failed miserably. In his mind it was him and Charlotte coming down here each weekend. Taking the drive down to the coast and walking along the beach. It was their kids he saw playing in the backyard.

He had to stop these fanciful ideas. Essentially this was a business arrangement between the two of them. Sleeping together would be a side benefit, but he couldn't think about playing happy home with her. Nor could he think about giving up on the dream of getting the oil out of this piece of land. It had always been his end goal. Even that last weekend with his high school buddies before heading off to college, he'd bragged to them about what he would do with the land once he got ahold of it.

Could he ask Charlotte to advise him on the best way to protect the surrounding lands? He knew it was a great hunting spot, so he didn't want to affect the animals. But Gage didn't think she'd take him up on his offer. Not when it was her land he was planning to partially destroy with his rigs.

"Did I send you off to sleep?" she asked.

He snuggled in and buried his face in her hair. "No. I was just thinking about other things. Tell me what you'd do to the house."

"I'd paint the outside. I like the color, so I'd just give it a fresh coat to bring it back to life. Then I'd renovate the kitchen. But I wouldn't tear it out and make it into a modern-looking kitchen like the stainless-steel and granite one in your apartment." She sighed. "I would maybe just re-stain the cupboards. They looked in pretty good condition when I cleaned them today. I would replace the counters with white quartz and get a big farmer's sink and paint the walls a light yellow. I always thought I'd like a yellow kitchen."

"Yellow is a good color. And I agree about the kitchen cupboards. Maybe change out the hardware to brighten it up, too."

He could feel a yawn take over her body. Talking was helping her to relax. But he wasn't about to suggest she go back to her room. Now that he had her in his arms, he wasn't planning on letting her go that easily.

"What would you do in the living room?" he inquired.

"Oh, that room would be bright and welcoming. I wouldn't have a television in there, though. That room would be where you could sit by the fire and read a book when it's raining. There's the other room on the other side of the kitchen that I would make into the family room. I would probably look at tearing down the wall between those two rooms so it would create an open plan concept and I could watch the kids while I cooked." She yawned again. "It would be perfect."

"It sounds like it. Is life turning out how you wanted it, Red?"

Gage had thought she'd fallen asleep as the silence dragged between them after his question. He was about to move to check when she spoke.

"In some ways it has and in other ways it hasn't."

"What do you mean?"

"Well, I wanted to work overseas and I'm doing that. One day I thought I'd have my own home, but inheriting it wasn't how I thought it would come about. And you already know what I thought about marriage."

Yeah, he did. He didn't like being a blot on her marriage copybook, but there was no going back now.

"There's still time to get your dream marriage and your dream home."

"True." A yawn racked her body, and he tightened his hold on her.

"Why don't you go to sleep now?"

"Okay." She snuggled into him and his dick appreciated the movement. "Thanks, Cowboy."

"Anytime, Red." He shifted his hips so he was nudging her ass with his hard length. He closed his eyes, and his last thought was that he'd never be able to sleep.

Chapter 18

Gage opened the door to his condo, allowing Charlotte to enter before him. The drive back from Sweet Ridge had been fairly quiet, with both of them lost in their own thoughts.

He spied the object of his thoughts as she placed it on the coffee table in his living room. He still couldn't explain why the thought of unlocking the box freaked him out so much. He thought he'd deciphered the initials entwined into the etched flower stems. To him they looked like a *J* and an *L*. The *J* could stand for *Jack*, but his mom's name was Denise.

Gavin and Grayson had been no help when he'd shown them the box at lunch. Neither one had recognized it, saying they couldn't recall seeing it in their mom's bedroom. Until he checked to see if the key opened the box, the mystery would remain.

"Are you okay?" Charlotte asked.

He pulled her into a one-arm hug and kissed the top of her head. "Yeah, just tired."

"That box is still bothering you, isn't it? Why don't you go get the key? Putting it off isn't going to make the concern go away. At least after opening it, you'll have some sort of an answer."

"I suppose you're right."

She tapped him lightly on the chest. "Now you're getting the hang of married life."

He looked at her quizzically. "What do you mean by that?"

"Well, it's simple, really. Your wife is always right. You keep remembering that, we'll have smooth sailing in our marriage."

Gage laughed, easing some of the tension. "Well, we'll just see if that's true."

A tug on his arm reminded him that he still had hold of Oil Slick. Bending down, he released the cat from her leash and she darted off around the apartment.

"You know, sometimes I wonder if being an animal isn't the way to go," he mused.

"Why do you say that?"

"Well, your biggest concern is usually when you're going to be fed. As a cat or even a dog, you get to sleep or play all day. You get endless cuddles, and someone is always cleaning up after you. You never have to worry about where your next paycheck is going to come from. Or whether or not you'll lose your house. Life can be pretty stress-free being a pet."

"I suppose that's true." Then she looked at him. "Unless, of course, you live in a house where, when you get a little older, the novelty of having a new puppy or kitten wears off and you start to get ignored. Like everything in this lottery we call life, you can draw the good numbers or you can draw the really shitty numbers. You've just got to make the most of the numbers you're given."

That was true. Some of the kids he'd seen while working on a rig off the coast of Brazil fit that philosophy. When he'd gotten some time to go into the nearby town, he'd been shocked at the way some people lived. But one thing remained with him. No matter what their living conditions, the kids, even with their dirty T-shirts and shorts, were so happy with their lot in life. They thought they'd hit the jackpot. It was only him who had found it surprising they could be so happy.

And here he was, a grown man, getting freaked out by a little box.

"You're right. I'm going to get the key."

Charlotte kissed him on the cheek. "I'll see what I can find to make for dinner."

He watched her walk away toward the kitchen, his body buzzing with awareness from her brief kiss. They hadn't really shared many hot kisses, even though he and his body were aching to take their relationship to the next level. He had to control the urge to follow her, pull her back in his arms, and kiss her until the next logical step was to find themselves tangled up in his sheets.

Gage shook his head, trying to rid himself of the erotic images. He walked into his bedroom and went over to his dresser to retrieve the key from the small top drawer.

The cold metal warmed in his hand. He lifted it up to the light and studied its shape. The more he looked, the more confident he felt that the key would fit the box.

Closing his fingers around it, he strode out of his room and back to the living room, where the box still sat on the middle of the coffee table. Two glasses of wine and a platter with some Guac Olé guacamole and corn chips sat innocently next to it.

Charlotte returned to the room. “You have the key?”

He held out his hand and opened his clenched fingers.

She nodded and sat on the couch, waiting for him to join her. With slow, measured steps, he walked to the couch and sat down. He put the key on the table in front of the box.

“It’s going to fit,” he murmured.

With a rustle of fabric Charlotte moved to align herself against his side, her hand sliding onto his thigh. Without thinking, he placed his own hand over hers.

“You ready?”

“I think so.” He lifted their hands and pressed his lips into the fleshy part of her palm. He then reached over and grabbed both the key and the box, placing the items on his lap. With Charlotte sitting close to him, lending him her strength, he knew he could face whatever the contents in the box were.

“Here goes.”

Gage pushed the key into the lock. It slid in easily. He felt Charlotte’s breath tickle his cheek. With a twist of his wrist, the key turned and the lock disengaged.

“It worked,” she whispered.

For a moment he didn't move. Then he started to laugh at the ridiculousness of the whole thing.

"What so funny?" she asked.

"This. Us. Everything. It hit me the second I released the lock. I'm making a soap-opera drama out of opening a lock. If this were being recorded for a show, I'd be in the running for an Emmy."

Charlotte giggled beside him. "We are being rather melodramatic. Just open the damn lid, then we can eat."

He did as she suggested. He looked into the box. Well, great, it was just another pile of letters. Probably as meaningless as the letters and photos Gavin had found in the safe-deposit box. He lifted them out and replaced the box onto the table.

"Okay, so this isn't what I was expecting."

Charlotte reached out and took the top one. "I wonder who they belong to. There's no address or name on the front or the back of the envelopes."

"I've no idea." On a whim he picked up the box again and pressed the base.

"Are you looking for a false bottom or something?"

"Yes, there isn't one." Instead of putting the box back on the table, he laid it at his feet so he could have room to spread the letters out on the table. What was the significance of the letters, and were they part of the clue to his father's note to him?

Charlotte put the letter she held back onto the pile. "Are you going to open them?"

That was the sixty-four-thousand-dollar question. He could be invading someone's privacy. Yet they had been found in the house on the land that once belonged to his father and that now belonged to Charlotte.

"You should probably open them," he said finally.

"Why?"

"Because they were found on your property. Essentially the box and the contents belong to you."

"But you're the one who owns the key that unlocks the box. And really, Cowboy, you need to read them, so quit being a big girl's blouse and start reading."

A buzzer sounded in the distance and Charlotte stood up. "That will be dinner. Take the box into the dining room and you can read them while you eat."

"Okay," he said.

Once in the dining room, he took Charlotte's advice to just read the letters. He grabbed the top letter, and a very faint fragrance tickled his nose, like the paper had been sprayed with perfume before it had been sent.

To my sweet Jack,

I'm writing this letter because I can't believe what I'm feeling is not a dream. I pinch myself and I don't wake up. It is real. And writing it down makes it even more real. I had the most wonderful time last night. I hope you did, too.

Until next time...

"What does it say?" she asked as she placed a steaming plate of pasta in a creamy sauce next to him.

"It looks like it's a love letter." He held it out to her.

He took a mouthful of the pasta while he watched Charlotte scan the letter. A sweet smile and a dreamy expression broke out over her face.

"It sure does, and it's almost like this letter was written after a first date."

Gage nodded and kept shoveling the food into his mouth. He finished off his dinner quickly and then extracted the next letter from its envelope. No scent drifted up from this one, and he immediately recognized the scrawl.

"This one's from Dad."

"What does it say?"

Gage began to read out loud.

My darling, sweet girl,

If it is a dream, then I'm dreaming with you. I never wanted the night to end, but sadly it had to. I've never smiled or laughed so much in my life. I can't wait to see you again. I hope you don't think me forward in asking if you are free Saturday afternoon? I will be waiting by the tree where we first met.

Until Saturday...

Jack

"Oh, Gage, this is beautiful."

Huh? Were women automatically programmed at birth to think love letters were so fascinating? There didn't seem to be anything special about the two notes he'd just read. "I'm afraid I don't follow you."

She reached across the table and touched his hand. "Don't you see? It's the start of your parents' romance. It sounds like love at first sight. Do you know how special that is? Nothing could be more romantic than that."

The dreamy expression came back over Charlotte's face, mixed this time with a little wistfulness.

"Do you believe in love at first sight?" he asked.

"I don't know. Maybe. I know my parents do. Do you?"

"I don't think so. Besides, we don't know how long it was between when my parents first met until their first date. It could've been a week or a month before Dad summoned up the courage to ask Mom out. If you noticed, the letters aren't dated."

The lightness in her face died a little, and he felt like a jerk for extinguishing that flame of romance within her.

She stood and collected the plates. "I'm going to take these through to the kitchen, and then I think I might go to bed. I'm a little tired."

She was up and out of the dining room before he could catch his breath. His hand hovered over another letter. He didn't pick it up. What was the point? The key he'd been left with, the key that supposedly led to happiness, led instead to a box of letters—and heartache. His father had never married after their mom had died. Had Jack Cooper been happy raising three boys by himself? Or had he been heartbroken that the woman he'd loved had been taken from him?

Gage put the useless letters back in the box. He wasn't going to get his answer from reading them. And he was sure they weren't going to answer his question of why the land now belonged to Charlotte and not him.

"Dad, seriously, what are you trying to tell me? What am I supposed to do with these letters?"

Chapter 19

Charlotte rolled over again, trying to get comfortable. The bed felt too big. Could one night spent sleeping in Gage's arms make it impossible for her to sleep alone? She'd been sleeping alone for most of her life. Even when she'd been in a semi-serious relationship, she'd been able to sleep apart from the person. Why was tonight so much harder to fall asleep?

Throwing the covers off in disgust, she got up and padded out to the kitchen. She pulled open the fridge and grabbed the carton of milk. She filled a glass and wandered over to the window. She opened the blinds a little to look out over the city. At this time of night she expected the streets to be empty, but there were still quite a few cars driving around.

Gage's reflection joined hers in the glass.

"Can't you sleep either?"

"It would seem that way," she responded tartly.

A light chuckle. "Yeah, that was kind of a dumb question."

Charlotte drained the rest of the milk before turning to face him. "So, why can't you sleep?"

He shrugged his shoulders. He was shirtless and he was breathtaking. The hard labor working on the rigs had defined his abs so that he had a nice six-pack. And no doubt regular gym work maintained the look. She gripped the glass a little tighter. What she wanted to do was reach out and touch him.

"I don't know. Just a lot on my mind, I guess."

She walked over to the sink, rinsed the glass, and placed it on the counter. "Did you read any more letters?"

"No. I didn't see much point. I'm not sure I want to read too much about my parents' romance. I might find out things I won't be able to forget. And I don't think they're going to give me the answers I want."

She opened her mouth and then closed it again. It wasn't her business what he decided to do with the letters. They looked at each other for endless minutes. Her body prickled with desire to kiss away the lines of disappointment on his face. If she didn't get out of here fast, she'd find herself giving in to the urge. Sleeping with Gage would change the boundaries of their relationship. She'd been the one to say the marriage was a business arrangement only, although it was getting harder and harder to keep her hands off her husband.

Charlotte pushed off the edge of the counter. It was time to get out of the kitchen, because the heat was becoming intense. "Well, I think I might try to see if I can get some sleep. It's going to be a long day tomorrow at work if I don't."

She brushed past Gage, averting her eyes from having one last look at his impressive chest. She hadn't gone an inch past him when his hand shot out and gripped her arm. Before she had time to think, she found herself up against that hard chest.

She looked up at him, ready to ask what he was doing, when his lips crashed down on hers. As his lips roved over hers, demanding a response, she gave it to him by opening her mouth. She wrapped her arms around his neck, her fingers playing with the thick strands of his hair.

Her neck fell back as he nipped his way from her lips to her jaw to the hollow of her collarbone. He scooped her up in his arms and carried her to his room, where he laid her on the bed before joining her.

"We shouldn't be doing this, Gage," she whispered. "It will only complicate things."

"It's too late, things are already complicated. This is what we should've done on our wedding night. This is as inevitable as breathing. And it's so simple, Red. I want you, and I think you want me, too."

She closed her eyes as his hand traced a line down her body, between her breasts, stopping just above the small sleep shorts she was wearing. His touch was gentle and perfect. She grabbed his hand and opened her eyes to look at him. "Yes. Everything you said is true. I want this. I want you."

He groaned and gathered her close, kissing her once again. Her hands roamed over his back, his muscles contracting beneath her fingertips, his skin so warm she was sure she was about to burst into flames.

When his hands gripped the hem of her top, she relinquished her hold on him so that she could lift her arms up to allow him to remove it.

"Oh yes." The words hissed out of her as Gage palmed her breasts. He rolled her nipples between his thumb and forefinger. Heat built up inside of her, and her hips moved against him. She needed to feel him, skin on skin. Her hands to went to the waistband of his shorts and pulled them down. His erection sprang out and bumped against her thigh.

He was right. This was what she'd been wanting since their first kiss.

"You're so beautiful, Red." He interspersed his words with kisses on first one breast then the other, playing and sucking on her nipples. She moaned in pleasure. If he kept this up, she'd orgasm just from him playing with her breasts.

Her own hands set out on their adventure, tracing the bumps of his spine until she reached the curve of his ass.

As she went to squeeze it, Gage moved, removing the taut flesh from her reach. "Not fair," she complained and bit his shoulder.

"Ouch. You're going to pay for that, Red."

"Really, what are you going to do, Cowboy?"

"This," he said, licking his way down her body until he found the top of her curls.

Her stomach muscles clenched in anticipation of his first touch at her core. As his tongue swiped her slick folds, she cried out. All coherent thought left her mind as he pleasured her with his tongue, stroking in and out of her, building the tension inside of her body. She gripped the sheets and lifted her hips to give him better access.

"Please, Gage," she whimpered as he stopped.

"What is it you want?"

"Oh God, I want you, Gage. Inside me. Over me. I need you."

He reached over and opened his bedside table drawer. "Your wish is my command." He pulled out a condom, ripped the foil, and rolled it on. He changed his position so that he rested his hard cock between her thighs. He nudged at her entrance. "Look at me."

She raised her eyes to connect with his. He leaned down and kissed her. She could taste herself on his lips. It only turned her on more.

Charlotte lifted her hips, feeling his head nudging her entrance. "Now, Gage."

His response was to start a slow, torturous slide into her. She bit her lip to stop herself from crying out at his possession. He then pulled out and entered again, this time all the way.

"Oh yes. Yes. Yes." It became her personal mantra as he increased his rhythm. Her orgasm built until it burst through her with a force she'd never felt before. She called out his name to mingle with his cry of "Charlotte" as he came inside of her.

When he collapsed on top of her, she welcomed his weight. He quickly rolled over, taking her with him. He feathered her face with soft kisses.

"You okay?" he asked.

She snuggled into him. "Mmm-hmmm."

"Sleep, Red."

Yes, she could sleep now. Lying in Gage's bed, in his arms—it was the perfect place to be.

• • •

Charlotte tried to move but couldn't. She stretched open an eyelid and came face-to-face with a black face and a little pink tongue lapping at a paw. She became aware that Oil Slick was only part of the reason she couldn't move. A heavy, hairy leg rested over the top of one of hers and an arm firmly anchored her around her waist.

Gage.

She and Gage had made love. Not once, but three times. Her body ached deliciously, but her mind ached in a completely different way.

What have I done?

As wonderful as it had been exploring Gage's body and allowing him to explore hers, as she'd feared, it added another complication to their already-complicated relationship. What happened in this bed had changed the parameters of their arrangement. They couldn't go back to having just a business arrangement. How on earth was she going to go back to sleeping on her own now?

Charlotte normally prided herself on her levelheadedness, but last night she had been anything but reasonable.

"I can feel you thinking," Gage muttered against her neck, his breath tickling the fine hairs. Her nipples peaked and heat suffused her body.

She was in so much trouble.

She needed to get out of here. Charlotte made a move to first get Oil Slick off her and then to pull the covers back so she could slip out.

Gage had other ideas, though, and he pulled her back until she curved into his body, his morning erection nudging her butt.

"I don't regret anything that happened last night," he started. "But I have a feeling you do."

What could she say? She could try to deny it, but what would be the point? It was the truth. She did regret sleeping with Gage—even though it was the best sex she'd ever had in her life.

"We shouldn't have done this, Gage."

His fingers began to draw patterns on her belly, causing her muscles to jump with every touch. There was no way he couldn't feel it, too.

"Why not? We're husband and wife."

"Yes, but it was supposed to be in name only. A business transaction. You get the land, I get a green card. No sleeping together to blur the lines. Now those lines are completely blurred."

"We agreed on that before we knew we had to be married for at least two years."

Indignation made her roll around and pull herself out of his embrace. "Are you telling me you slept with me because you're stuck with me for two years now?"

He ran a hand through his hair. She recalled the texture of it from her own exploration of it last night.

"No, I slept with you because I want you. Because I've wanted you since before we even got married. With us being married for at least two years, would you have been happy to sleep in separate rooms the whole time? And you do realize that as part of the process to obtain your green card, we could be interviewed here, in our condo, by the Immigration Department? What are they going to say if they see we're sleeping in separate rooms, or even are awkward around each other?" He shrugged his shoulders. "This way, when and if they do a home visit, there will be no awkwardness between us. All things considered, sleeping together actually enhances our chances of convincing the Immigration Department that our marriage isn't a scam. We all win in the end."

While his words made sense to her, Charlotte didn't know how she was going to be able to keep her heart out of the relationship. His flippant attitude about it all annoyed her, as well. It hurt to think he could approach this change in their relationship so casually. Of course, for a man it wasn't hard to separate emotions from sex. How many times had she heard girls in the office in Sydney bemoaning the fact that the guy they were currently seeing wouldn't take that next step and commit to them? The guys were happy to have a warm body in their beds but then still go out with their mates. She'd never pegged Gage to be a sleep-and-run kind of guy, and she'd hoped she was right.

She couldn't deny how tempted she was to throw caution to the wind and agree to the change in their relationship status. But then she'd end up being like those girls she'd rolled her eyes at as they'd cried into their coffee in the break room. How was it that guys could so easily compartmentalize their lives? Sex and emotions in separate boxes in their minds and their hearts.

"I don't know, Gage. I don't think it's the best idea."

His response was to lean over, push her hair to the side, and start to nuzzle her neck, to kiss her in the spot under her chin she'd had no idea was so sensitive.

A moan escaped her, even though she tried to bury it.

"You don't play fair."

He chuckled against her neck. "When I want something, I do everything necessary to get it." He kissed her softly then. Her insides churned in anticipation of what might follow.

She ripped her lips away from his and looked into his desire-laden eyes. "Yes."

"Yes to what?" he asked. He was making her say the words out loud.

"Yes to altering the terms of our marriage. Yes to moving into your bedroom. Yes to making this marriage more than one on paper only."

"Good." He grinned wildly, setting her heart to fluttering in five different directions.

Oh boy, she was in so much trouble.

Chapter 20

Gage studied the wooden box that sat in the middle of the coffee table. He hadn't looked at its contents since the night he and Charlotte first made love, even though she'd told him he should. He kept putting it off and distracting Charlotte with a kiss that always led them to his bedroom. It had been incredible to share his bed with her during the past week. Tonight it would be lonely in his bed without her there.

He looked down when something nudged his leg. Oil Slick was pacing in front of him, brushing up against him with every turn she made. He no longer took her to work every day, as she seemed to have gotten used to the condo and no longer tried to destroy it. He would deny it loudly if anyone said anything, but he did miss having the cat in the office. Maybe he'd take her to work with him tomorrow.

"You missing Red, too?" he asked the cat as it jumped up on the couch next to him. "She'll be back tomorrow. Shall I cook a special dinner for her? Dinner for two in bed? No cats allowed."

The cat meowed plaintively as if she knew she was not being included.

His cell rang and Charlotte's face lit up his screen.

"Hey there, Mrs. Cooper. You giving them all sorts of hell?"

His body went from zero to aroused in less than a second when she chuckled at his comment.

"I save my hell-giving for you," she responded.

"I can believe that."

"I can always hang up if that's what you really want."

"And break Oil Slick's heart by not talking to her? You wouldn't do that."

He could envision her shaking her head and rolling her eyes at his antics. "Are you sure it would be Oil Slick who would be upset?"

He sobered up, all humor gone. "No, I would be upset if you hung up. So, how about you tell me what's happening. How's Shreveport? How'd the meeting go?"

"Shreveport is fine. The meeting went well. They seem to be open to my suggestions, but then again, what people say in a meeting is often different from what they follow through with."

"What do you mean?"

"Well, think back on what you said to me when I first proposed the changes to the way you prepared your Midland site for drilling. You didn't think it was necessary to consider a different entrance point to protect the expanse of trees that had stood there for over a hundred years. You just about bit my head off through the phone line with your adamant refusal to follow my suggestions."

Gage laid his head against the back of the couch. Yeah, he'd been a total dick when he'd first come in contact with Charlotte. "True, but I am learning that your suggestions and ideas won't compromise my operations too much."

"This is new. You haven't mentioned to me you're reconsidering."

"Yeah, I didn't want to say anything until I'd spoken to the surveyor and confirmed that the new entrance point would be viable."

"I told you it would be. I even said it would save you money, if you remember."

"I remember. I should learn to listen a bit more, shouldn't I?"

"Yes, you should."

Oil Slick jumped off the couch, and Gage swiveled so he could stretch out on it. He'd had enough of talking about work. Instead he used his sexy bedroom voice, or so Charlotte called it, to say, "What are you wearing, Red?"

His shorts tented a little more in anticipation of what he hoped would come next. "I'm wearing my navy suit, sans jacket and shoes."

Gage bit back a groan. He knew exactly what outfit Charlotte was talking about. The jacket nipped in at her waist, emphasizing the curve of her generous bust. The skirt was snug over her ass and stopped just above her knees. He'd taken one look at her putting it on earlier in the week and hadn't been able to control himself. They had both been late for work that day. But for him, it was totally worth it.

"No wonder you won everyone over. You look so hot in that suit. I wish you were here, though. I'd help you out of it."

If he wasn't mistaken, he heard a groan. "You wouldn't get any argument out of me. In fact…"

Gage heard some rustling and then what he thought sounded like a zipper sliding down. He closed his eyes and let his free hand go to his shorts, stroking his hard length through the fabric.

"I'm now sans skirt," she whispered. "And I'm on the bed."

"You want to do this, Red?"

"How about we Facetime? I need to see you."

Oh yes, now they were talking. She might not be lying next to him. He might not be able to touch her. But he could still make her come, and it was going to be one of the hottest things he ever did.

•••

Gage climbed into bed, well sated. Who knew Charlotte could be so wicked and wild? He liked it. He liked her. A lot.

Getting through the two years of marriage to help her get a green card wasn't going to be an issue. And when the two years were up and she had her residency, they could think about their next step then. There was no point planning beyond that. Who knew what tomorrow would bring?

But tonight, after finishing his conversation with Charlotte, he knew it was time to read a couple more letters.

He settled himself comfortably in the bed and reached for the box. He suspected the letters had been placed in the box in the order of when they'd been written and received. But he'd procrastinated enough. It was time to stop pussyfooting around and just open the next damn envelope.

Like the first letter, the scent of perfume tickled his nostrils.

To my sweet Jack,

I'm lying in my room looking at the lovely flowers you gave me today on our picnic. Again, you turned my dull life into something so magical. I keep thinking that it can't be possible. This can't be real. But it is. I constantly ask myself, how could a man as successful and handsome as you be interested in me? I'm a nobody. I'm not pretty or smart. I can barely make ends meet. What do you see in me, Jack? The answer scares me, but I need to know.

I want to thank you, also, for being a true gentleman. If, at any time in the future, you'd like to be a little bit non-gentlemanly, I won't say no.

I hope that I can see you again soon.

Gage smiled. Jack Cooper was a gentleman, and he had instilled that into his sons. Sometimes Gage forgot the way Dad would lecture him about his behavior toward girls. Would Dad be happy with the way he was treating Charlotte? Would he be proud of his youngest son? Gage would never know, but a part of him hoped Dad could see that he was trying to do the right thing by Charlotte, that he was trying to do something right in his life after letting his dad down so badly by being kicked out of college and blowing the dream of a career in the NFL.

He slipped the paper back into the envelope and placed it facedown on top of the other two he'd read. He didn't want to lose the order they were in. He had to admit, he was surprised his mother seemed so unsure of herself. From what little Gavin and Grayson had told him, Denise Cooper had presided over the house like a queen. Maybe Dad's love had given her the strength she needed to blossom into the woman she was supposed to become.

He grabbed the next letter.

My darling, sweet, beautiful girl,

Yes, you read that right, I said "beautiful" because you are. You are more beautiful than the sunset on a hot summer day, more beautiful than the rarest flower. I get lost in your stunning eyes. I could stare into them all day and be satisfied. Maybe I can turn the question onto you. What do you see in me? There's nothing special about me. Maybe that's why we work so well together. We bring out the best in each other.

I, too, had the most wonderful time today. I didn't want it to end. It was the hardest thing for me to say good-bye to you. When can I see you again? I don't know why you don't want me to come and pick you up. But I won't pressure you. And maybe next time I won't be so gentlemanly.

Can I see you on Saturday night? Dinner at Betty Lou's Diner?

I await your response.

Until then…

To my sweet Jack,

Nothing thrills me more than when I see your note waiting for me, and now in a beautiful wooden box. I'm scared to think too much about the combined hearts, but I must admit my heart is becoming combined with yours. I find myself thinking constantly about you, about our upcoming date on Saturday night. I can't wait to see you, and then I'll tell you what I see in you. By the way, that's a yes to your dinner invitation.

I must go now. I know that you will find this in our special box. In our special place. I will place it as carefully as you did to protect it and the notes we share.

Until Saturday…

So, his father had this box made to hold the letters. Gage could accept the romantic gesture of writing notes to each other, but as the only way to communicate with each other surprised him. Why didn't they talk on the telephone? And why didn't his father call his mother by her name?

He wasn't planning to read anymore, but he picked up another one.

My darling, sweet Nora,

It is early Sunday morning when I am writing this. I know you are getting ready to go to church, so you may not check the box for another couple of days, but I know that I must write down what is in my heart to you.

I know we've only known each other for a short time. You told me you were scared about the combined hearts on the box. But I am very sure of my feelings, and I fear I may have scared you last night with my declaration.

I want you to know that I am a patient man. I will wait for you. I will wait an eternity for you. Please don't be frightened away because I blurted out that I love you.

I hope that in a few days' time I can go to our special hiding spot and find a return letter from you. If there is no letter, I will not despair. I will go to our special tree on Saturday afternoon at 3 p.m. and wait. I will wait all night for you. I hope that you will be there.

All my love,

Jack

Gage read the letter twice. He went to pick up the phone to call, Gavin but stopped when he looked at the time. It really was too late to call.

Nora.

He didn't recognize the name at all. A yawn racked his body. Was there someone in town called Nora when was growing up?

He didn't think so, but then again he could be wrong. The more he tried to think, the less luck he had in extracting the information from the dark recesses of his mind.

The love Dad felt for this Nora woman was jumping off the letters. But he still couldn't see the correlation between the note Dad had left him and the letters he was reading. He also felt a twinge of guilt at how different his relationship with Charlotte was and the relationship between Jack Cooper and the woman in the note.

Warning bells were clamoring inside of him: No good would come of reading any more of these notes. So many people around town used to say that the love Jack had for Denise, the mother of his sons, so encompassed him that he remained single for the rest of his life, unable to find another love as beautiful as the love they'd shared. He wondered if it was true at the beginning of his parents' relationship, but he wasn't so sure it was true by the time his mom died in the car accident. He might have only been five at the time of her death, but he knew he had heard his parents arguing when they thought no one was around.

God, did it even matter what sort of relationship his parents shared? People fell in and out of love all the time—just look at the divorce rates. People would write notes, or e-mails now, similar to the ones his father had written, claiming that the person they were writing to was the one love of their life, but a couple of years down the track, the love was gone and all they had was a shell of a marriage. Maybe Jack had thought he loved this Nora to distraction, but then he didn't end up with her. Jack had married Denise. Not Nora.

Gage groaned out loud in frustration. He had so many questions, and he couldn't ask anyone because it was so damn late. He would have to call his brothers in the morning. No, he needed to ask them face-to-face. He and Charlotte hadn't made plans to head to Sweet Ridge this weekend, but now it had become a necessity. He only hoped the trip wouldn't unravel the fabric of the lives that he and his brothers had always known.

Chapter 21

Excitement built inside of Charlotte the closer they got to Sweet Ridge. She couldn't wait to see the house again. Gage had told her he'd arranged for some furniture to be delivered so that they could have a couch to sit on and a proper bed to sleep in.

But one glance at Gage revealed the tension around his mouth, and his hands gripped the steering wheel tightly. He looked like he was about to face the executioner's chair. He hadn't looked like this even when they got married. Was he nervous about the meeting with the immigration people that was looming at the end of next week? He'd been relaxed when they'd met with the lawyer.

Stop dithering, just ask the man. For goodness' sake, you had Facetime sex with him. He's not going to blow you off now.

"Hey, Cowboy," she started softly. "Everything okay?" She placed her hand on his thigh.

"What?"

Apprehension skidded down her spine. Ever since her return from Shreveport, Gage had seemed distracted. Although that hadn't stopped him from making love to her at every opportunity. She would never forget how happy she'd been when she'd walked out of the airport to find him waiting for her. She shivered as she remembered the kiss he gave her. They hadn't even been able to make it to the bedroom of the condo. He'd taken her hard and fast against the hallway wall, and she'd loved every minute of it.

Perhaps he was concerned about seeing his brothers again, even though everything seemed to be okay when they'd left the last time they'd visited. She knew he'd spoken to Gavin and Grayson since their last visit. Whether she came up in the conversation or not, Gage never told her.

And did it really matter if they had discussed her? They were married, and there was nothing his brothers could do about it. Just like there was nothing she could do about her growing appreciation for the man Gage truly was. Spending time with him, she'd discovered he wasn't the overbearing, pain-in-the-ass oil man she'd first thought him to be. No one who could talk to a cat the way he talked to Oil Slick was an unfeeling jerk.

"I asked if everything was okay. You seem a little preoccupied. You're not worried about how Gavin and Grayson will treat me, are you?"

"Um, no. No, not at all," he repeated with a little more force. "I'm just—I've got a meeting early next week with regard to a new parcel of land I'm looking at acquiring. The deal is, you know … well, it could be a little tricky. So, I, uh, need to make sure I've got my mind in the right place, as this owner could prove difficult to bring around to my way of thinking."

Was he telling the truth? Or was he keeping something from her? His hesitations were out of character. Either the deal really was important or he was lying to her.

"Are you sure that's it, Gage? Is there something you're not telling me?"

"No, Red. It really is what's going through my mind. But it's the weekend. I don't want to talk about work."

She studied him a little longer. Did she want to push it and potentially spoil their weekend? No, she'd make a mental note to bring it up to him on Sunday night. They always had brief *how-was-your-day* type of discussions. But she'd noticed Gage glancing more regularly at his phone the last couple of days. Perhaps he did have a big deal he was concerned about.

He had steered most of their evening conversations around the house and what she wanted to do to it decorating and renovation wise. With each conversation they'd shared about the house, hope had begun to blossom inside of her. Hope that Gage was reevaluating his plan to mine for oil. Hope that he could see that house as their future vacation home before becoming their permanent residence. Hope that he was starting to care a little about her and her hopes and dreams.

"This deal is one you can't discuss with me? Maybe I could help you."

His thigh muscles tensed briefly beneath her fingers. "Thanks for the offer, but it's best I deal with this alone. Until I know for sure. After that, then, yes, I'd appreciate your help."

"Okay, but if you change your mind, I'll be happy to help out."

"I know, Red. Thank you." He picked up her hand from his thigh and brought it to his lips. He placed a soft kiss on it. The smallest of touches, but enough to start a slow burn inside of her.

He kept hold of her hand the rest of the drive to the house. The action pushed away the doubts she'd begun to dream up.

Charlotte's breath sighed out as the house came into view. "This really is the perfect way to spend the weekend. I love Houston, but the constant stream of traffic and people going everywhere can be exhausting. I think I may introduce a no cell phone rule down here."

"Good luck with that," he responded as he pulled the car to a stop. "That would mean you couldn't send your mom texts every day to tell her what you're doing."

"Well, maybe it would be a one hour in the morning and one hour in the evening allowance." She unclipped her seat belt. "That's fair, don't you think?"

"We can discuss it later. First"—he waggled his eyebrows at her and she knew exactly what he was about to say next—"I think we should go inside and test out the new bed." He leaned over the console and lightly gripped her chin between his fingers. "It's been too long since I've been able to hold you."

Before she could dispute it, his lips possessed hers, and any objection she had to his plan was quickly forgotten. Her hands roamed his shoulders, and down his muscled back until she could grip the hem of his T-shirt. Gaining access to his bare back, she slipped her hands under his shirt.

"You feel so good, Gage," she muttered against his lips. "Take me inside. You're right—we need to test out the new bed."

"Your wish is my command. Race you there."

Charlotte laughed as she jumped out of the car and then walked slowly to the front door. He couldn't get in without a key and she had it. Gage was already at the door, with Oil Slick sitting beside him. She had no idea how he was able to release the cat and get to the front door so quickly. He turned around and his eyes almost bugged out of his head when he caught on to the fact that she was coming up the walkway—slowly unbuttoning her blouse. She had no idea who she turned into when she was around Gage, but she loved it. She loved being able to be so free and open with Gage—her husband.

"You are one wickedly sexy lady." His lips crashed down on hers, his hands gripping her hips and pulling her hard up against him. He leaned back against the closed front door, giving them something solid to hold them upright.

It was lucky the house was not on the main street of Sweet Ridge or they'd be creating a scandal.

"Key," she mumbled against his lips. "Let me get the key."

"I've got this," he said as he fished out a key and unlocked the door. She looked at him in astonishment until she remembered that deliverymen had needed to have a way to get in to set up the furniture. Gage had organized everything because she'd been away. No wonder he wanted to race her to the door.

In a flash the door was open and she found herself flung over his shoulder, fireman-carry style. She would've complained, but this gave her an excellent view of his tight butt.

Oil Slick wandered in, looking at her human owners like they were the craziest people on earth.

Charlotte reached out and gave the front door a push to close it, then tapped him lightly on his denim-clad butt. "The view's not bad from down here, Cowboy."

A corresponding tap on her own butt made her laugh. "Likewise."

The door to the master bedroom stood open, but she didn't have a chance to take it all in. The moment they entered the room, Gage released his hold on her and started kissing her again. His hands were busy pushing off her open blouse. Her hands were just as busy divesting him of his shirt. Within seconds they were naked and on the bed, arms and legs entwined.

"I need you so badly," he said as he ripped open the condom he'd pulled from his jeans pocket before she'd flung the pants away.

"Me, too. Hurry."

He rolled the condom on and then he was entering her with one quick thrust. He paused before starting up a frantic rhythm she had no trouble meeting. Their hips slapped together as they both sought to drive each other crazy.

She was so close to climaxing. Gage only had to look at her to make her wet, and his wild kisses had intensified her desire for him.

The tension in her spine built and then fanned out across her back until it arrowed down to her core, where her orgasm crashed over her like a six-foot wave.

She called out his name, her body vibrating with the intensity of it. While her body still pulsed, Gage rolled them over and then she was riding him. Her head went back, and his hands on her hips guided her movements. Within seconds another orgasm built and exploded inside of her, and this time Gage called out her name as he reached his own release.

Charlotte collapsed on top of him, exhausted in a most pleasurable way, their ragged breathing the only sound in the room.

"It's safe to say the bed is comfortable," Gage said against her neck. The vibration from his voice sent another wave of sensations through her.

"I think you chose well. And, yes, it's much better to be on a solid mattress than one filled with air."

Gage shifted their positions so that they were lying on their sides face-to-face. She reached out and brushed away a lock of hair that had fallen over his forehead. "Apart from the business deal troubling you, is there anything else you want to tell me?"

He closed his eyes, and she wondered if he was going to avoid answering her question. But when he opened his eyes, she could read the confusion and sadness in them. Her body stilled, waiting to hear what he had to say.

"I read some more letters."

That wasn't what she'd been expecting him to say at all.

"And what did they say?"

"Enough for me to think the letters weren't written by my parents. Well, Dad wrote them, of course, but who he wrote them to wasn't Mom."

She propped her head up on her elbow, scooting a little closer to Gage so that their legs rested together. She had a feeling he needed to know she was there for him. "Why do you say that?"

"Because the last letter I read, my dad addressed it to 'my sweet, darling Nora.'"

"And that's not your mum's name?"

"No, Mom's name was Denise, and whenever Dad talked about her, he always referred to her as Denise. Never anything else. Certainly not Nora."

She could understand why finding the letters and discovering they weren't correspondence between his parents bothered Gage. Perhaps he'd taken to heart what she'd said the first night when they read a couple of the letters, that it was his chance to follow the romance between his parents. Now it seemed it wasn't.

Maybe her parents' story was worth sharing with Gage.

"Both of my parents had serious relationships before they found each other. But they both said that the moment their eyes locked, they knew no one else mattered to them. Maybe this Nora was an earlier relationship, and then when Jack met your mum, everything made sense and this Nora didn't matter anymore."

"You know I wish I could believe that."

"Why can't you?"

"Because Dad saved the letters. Whoever he was writing to, he loved her enough not to destroy them at the end of the relationship. You could see it in every word he wrote how much he cared. And whoever he wrote to, this Nora, she felt the same way."

"So I take it, this is the reason for our trip down here. Have you told your brothers anything about the letters yet?"

"You're right. Coming here, in part, was to see Gavin and Gray, but also I remembered what you said about spending weekends here. It seemed like a good habit to get into, and showing my brothers the letters was a bonus."

Little by little she was falling for Gage. The fact that he remembered their conversation about what she'd do if she kept the house—making it a weekend getaway—the man was as romantic as he claimed his father had been in the letters.

Charlotte leaned forward and kissed him on the lips. "You really are the best, Gage Cooper."

Chapter 22

Lunchtime on Saturday at the Silver Spurs was busy. Gage hadn't wanted to tell his brothers about the letters in the middle of a crowded bar, but it looked like he had no choice. They weren't in any position to entertain again at the house. After they'd arrived the previous evening, they'd spent the whole night in bed. He smiled at the memory of the jelly sandwiches he and Charlotte had had for dinner. That was all that had been in the fridge and the freezer.

"Do you have the letters?" Charlotte asked as they waited at the table for the others to arrive.

"In the car."

"Hopefully Gavin and Grayson will be able to help us solve the mystery of Nora."

"Yeah. I hope they'll be able to shed some light on it. I don't think there was anyone in town called Nora when we were growing up."

"It could've been someone before you were born. But you won't have long to wait." Charlotte inclined her head to the door. "Everyone's here."

Gage took a deep breath as his brothers and Macy walked toward them. He reached for Charlotte's hand. He liked touching her.

"Hey," he said as his brothers sat down. He noted Macy sat on the other side of Charlotte, giving her a hug before reaching over to squeeze his arm in greeting.

"Hey, bro, Charlotte," Grayson said. "Another weekend in Sweet Ridge. Soon you'll be moving down here."

Gage laughed at how close Grayson matched Charlotte's ideal plan—if she didn't sell the house to him. He hated to be the one to deny her dream, but the surveyor's report had come in just before they'd left for Sweet Ridge. He'd only glanced at it briefly, but from what he'd seen, there was more oil than he'd thought sitting underground on the land, just waiting for him to extract it. That oil would bring an influx of cash into his company that would help it remain in the black for a very long time. He knew he'd dodged a bullet on the way down when she asked him what he was worried about and how he fumbled over his words. He thought for sure she was going to push the issue. Relief washed over him when she had decided not to pursue the subject any further.

He figured he would pay her triple the true value of the land, and she'd be able to buy another property where she could build her dream vacation house. He knew that he might not be a part of that new property, but he would get over it. It wasn't like he was in love with Charlotte. But the thought of not waking up with her … of ruining her dream because he wanted to drill the land … he didn't like how that made him feel. But he also didn't want to give up on his own dream.

"Geez, Gage, are you daydreaming? I've never known you to be so vague. What's going on, man?"

Gage turned to Gavin. He had to admit he'd zoned out the moment his brothers had arrived. He physically shook his head to try to get some focus.

"Sorry, it's good to see you."

"Yeah, you, too. Are you sure everything is okay? How are you and Charlotte getting on? Must be difficult to be married to someone you barely know."

Gage glanced over to where Charlotte, Macy, and Grayson were chatting among themselves. He smiled. She really fit well into his life. "You'd think," he said to Gavin. "But I can honestly say that Charlotte is one of the better things in my life. I look forward to coming home to her. She was away for one night this week, and the condo seemed so quiet and lonely without her. I didn't like it."

But that could be his future when he took possession of the land.

Gavin slapped him on the back. "Oh man, you've got it bad."

Gage knew exactly what Gavin was talking about, but there was no way he was really in love with Charlotte. He cared. But no, it wasn't love.

"Whatever." A change of subject was needed. He didn't want to get into the nitty-gritty of his relationship with Charlotte. "Hey, Gray, I've got something to tell you and Gavin."

"You've finally decided oil is not for you, so you're going to come work at the plant and make a career out of peeling avocados again."

Gage laughed, remembering the summer he'd helped out at the factory. After one day of unsuccessfully peeling more avocados than successfully, Dad had dragged him over to the packing line, where Gage hoisted more boxes of guacamole into the back of a truck for delivery than he cared to remember. The only good thing about that summer was that lifting those boxes had built up his arm muscles and his abs, so he returned to school with a body the girls went crazy over and he enjoyed his best-ever high school football season. He ran more yards and got more catches than the other running backs on his team. As far as he knew, he still held the record at Sweet Ridge High. It had been that season that he had caught the eyes of many college football scouts. He'd had offers coming at him left, right, and center. But then he'd fucked it all up, because the people he thought were his friends turned out to be guys who were threatened by his talent and wanted him off the team. They'd gotten their wish, and he'd gotten his father's disappointment.

"Earth to Gage. Earth to Gage. Sheesh, Charlotte, what are you doing to this poor guy?" It was Grayson who commented this time.

Charlotte touched his face. "You okay, Cowboy?"

What that fuck was wrong with him, bringing up all these old memories best forgotten and acting like a loony flying away with the fairies every two minutes?

He turned his face and kissed Charlotte on the fleshy part of her palm. Her eyes widened in reaction. He sent her his *you-me-bed-later* look. "Yeah, I'm fine, Red. And Guac Olé's avocados are safe from my hands."

"Just as well," joked Gray. "I don't need any reason for my new partner to question my methods come September first. But you also had your best football season after that summer, if I recall."

"Football?" asked Charlotte. "That's right, Macy mentioned you'd played. How come you've never told me about it?"

"Long story."

He withstood Charlotte's questioning look. From the corner of his eye, he could see Grayson fidgeting. He should after opening that can of worms with his comment.

Gage wanted to call out Grayson for his comment, but he needed to stop avoiding what he really wanted to talk about with his brothers.

"So, the key Dad left me unlocked that box I found."

"What was inside?" Macy asked, leaning forward, an excited look on her face.

"Did you get a clue or an answer to what Dad's note meant?" Gavin asked.

"Or maybe an explanation from dear old Dad as to why he didn't give me all the shares to the company like he promised?" This from Grayson.

"I found a bunch of letters. No. And no." At the look of exasperation on his brothers' and Macy's faces, he decided to elaborate. "From what I can see, there is no explanation for Dad's actions with regard to the contents of his will or an answer to the note. The box contained love letters between Dad and some woman. I thought at first they were between Dad and Mom, but now I'm not so sure."

"Why do you say that?" asked Gavin.

Before he could answer, Meg, the Silver Spurs' head waitress, came up to the table. "Y'all want to order? You've been sitting here for ages and, well, it is a place of business, not a park bench."

They placed their orders, and when Meg walked away. Gage answered the question Gavin had asked before they were interrupted. "The first couple of letters, Dad addressed them to 'my darling, sweet girl,' which is why I thought they were to Mom. But her responses seemed a little out of character from what Mom was like. In the letters she was very unsure of herself."

"I may have been just nine when she died, but she always seemed so full of life, and there was no way she was shy or unsure," Gavin commented.

"As I said, at first I thought it was Mom," Gage said. "But then I read a few more letters and came across one Dad addressed to 'my darling, sweet Nora.' I didn't read any more after that one. I wanted to talk to you to see if the name rings a bell with either one of you. Did Dad ever call Mom 'Nora'?" Gage felt like he was grasping at straws.

"I don't think he did," Gavin responded. "Although I remember there was one time, toward the end of his cancer treatment, when he was in a lot of pain. The nurse gave him his shot and he muttered something. I asked him to repeat it and he said, 'Tell her I'm sorry. I'm sorry, Nora.'"

"You're shitting me. *Now* you're remembering this, Gavin?"

Gavin rolled his eyes. "Geez, Gage. I was dealing every day with Dad wasting away in front of me. I can't always remember everything we said or did."

Guilt assailed Gage. He'd been so busy running his business and going from rig to rig, only making the odd trip down to Sweet Ridge to see Dad, while Gavin cared for him every single day—even moving into the house with Dad. It was too late now to do anything to help, but it was never too late to say what Gavin's actions meant to him.

"Gavin, I'm sorry. You're right. I don't think I've said it, but thank you for what you did for Dad. I know it can't have been easy, and, well, I'm an ass for not having done more. I should've come down more often. Looked after Dad sometimes so you could go out and have a dinner or go on a date."

Gavin nodded his head in acknowledgment. "Thanks, bro. It's fine. Dad enjoyed your visits."

The words seemed hollow to Gage, like Gavin was just saying them to appease him. The guilt he'd thought he'd conquered about all the times he'd let his dad and family down reared its ugly head again.

"It's still not enough. I should've done more."

"Stop it, Gage," Gavin commanded. "I don't think you failed me or Dad. So don't take on guilt when you don't need to."

Gage nodded. The last thing he wanted to do was upset his brother.

"Thanks, Gavin."

"You're a good person, Gage Cooper." He shivered as Charlotte whispered the words in his ear. "Don't forget that."

He turned his head and kissed her, softly and sweetly. She responded to him straightaway, her nails digging into his thighs. His body stirred to life. He could never get enough of her. He pulled away and rested his forehead against hers and whispered, "I don't know about being a good person, but I try."

Gage waited for his brothers and Macy to give him a hard time when he turned his attention back to them, but all that greeted him was Gavin and Macy looking at them with a goofy grin on their faces. Grayson stared in the opposite direction, clearly letting him know that their public display of affection had embarrassed him.

He cleared his throat and tried to remember what had been happening before he kissed Charlotte.

Grayson saved him. "So it seems Dad might have been in love with someone before he and Mom got together? Is that what you're saying?"

"Seems that way."

"Okay, so what's the issue, then?" Grayson asked. "Doesn't it always happen? You fall in love. Fall out of love. Fall in love. Fall out of love. The circle of life and all that stuff." Grayson lifted his drink to his lips.

Gage muffled a groan when Charlotte elbowed him in his ribs. She had a smug *I-told-you-so* look on her face. He chuckled. "Yes, it's possible that this Nora could've been a former love of Dad's. But why would he keep all the letters if it was a love affair gone wrong? And why hide them away in a house he never visited?"

Grayson shrugged. "How should I know? Maybe he wanted to forget the love affair."

"No," Macy interjected. "You're wrong, Grayson. If you want to forget a love affair, you don't keep letters as mementos. You burn them or rip them up. Gage, did you say you had the letters she wrote to Jack as well as the ones he wrote to her?"

"Yeah. If I were a betting man, I'd say all the letters they wrote to each other are in the box."

Macy tapped her chin as she contemplated what he'd told her. "Why did Jack have all the letters, I wonder?"

He shrugged his shoulders. "No idea."

"Gavin, you said Jack mentioned Nora's name once when he was in pain. Was that the only time he mentioned it?" Charlotte asked the question he'd been about to ask.

"Well," Gavin started but stopped when Meg arrived at their table with their food. Her timing was impeccable at interrupting at the exact right moment. Gage drummed his fingers on the table. The moment Meg left their earshot, he leaned forward.

"You were saying, Gavin?"

"No, Dad didn't mention her again, but"—he looked over at Macy—"babe, do you remember when we cleaned out the drawers in Dad's desk in his home office, and we found that business card from a hotel in Houston—it had the name *Nora* written on the back, didn't it? It was tucked right at the back of the drawer."

Another thing Gavin was remembering after the fact. Gage couldn't believe his brother could be so vague. But then again, sometimes the littlest things you think wouldn't mean anything, were actually the most important.

"You're right," Macy said. "It was hard for Gavin to go through Jack's things," she explained to the brothers. "It's not surprising we didn't remember or make the connection straightaway."

Another thought hit Gage, one he couldn't believe he hadn't thought of until now. "What about those photos you found in the safe-deposit box, Gavin? You know, the ones with Dad and that woman. Do you suppose she could be Nora?"

"No idea," Gavin said.

"Maybe," Grayson responded.

As if by an unspoken agreement everyone turned their attention to their meals, and the conversation changed to subjects that had nothing to do with letters or hotel business cards or Dad's former love affairs.

Gage had to admit, he was a little relieved. He didn't know whether there were any answers in the letters about what went wrong with the love affair, but right now he didn't want to read any more of them.

Out of sight, out of mind could've been his dad's reason for hiding the box in the attic. Gage couldn't help but agree with his father if that was the case.

Chapter 23

Charlotte wiped her hands down her skirt as she and Gage sat in the immigration lawyer's waiting room.

"We've got this, Red. Don't worry." Gage's words should've reassured her, but she couldn't help but still be worried. They'd decided to keep the story they relayed to the officer as close to the truth as possible. They would see how the interview was going before they mentioned the land Jack had left her.

"I know, but still, you know it's a big thing, this interview. We have to make sure we're convincing." She kept her voice low so the receptionist couldn't hear their conversation.

"I can kiss you," he suggested. "We're pretty good at doing that. From memory, it always seems to calm you down. I promise I'll keep my hands on your elbows. Even though I'd rather be checking to see if you've got those sexy, stay-up stockings on again."

She laughed at the audacity of his words. "Steady yourself, Cowboy. And as to the stockings, well, if you're good, maybe I'll give you a little look—*after* the interview."

She bit her lip to stop herself from groaning out loud when Gage leaned over and nipped her ear before whispering, "I promise I'll be very good."

"Mr. and Mrs. Cooper? Mr. Slater will see you now."

"Saved by the receptionist," Gage joked as he stood and pulled her up with him.

Charlotte could only imagine what the receptionist was thinking about the way they were acting, but then again, perhaps it was a good thing. She had no idea whether the immigration officer would question any of the law firm's staff to confirm that the marriage was more than a "green card marriage."

They followed the receptionist down the hall. Instead of walking into an office, they found themselves in a boardroom. Charlotte's grip tightened around Gage's hand, her nerves coming back in full force.

"Good morning, Mr. and Mrs. Cooper. Please take a seat." The lawyer stood as they approached the table and pointed to the vacant chairs opposite him.

Gage held out a chair for her and as she sat, he squeezed her shoulder quickly before taking the seat next to her and reaching for her hand. She grabbed it like it was the lifeline she needed to prevent her from drowning.

"May I introduce you to Daphne Lewitsky from the Immigration Department? Today's meeting is just a preliminary discussion to review the application and for Ms. Lewitsky to meet you both."

Charlotte's tongue was stuck to the roof of her mouth. Even if she could speak, she had a feeling her words would be unintelligible, so she smiled and nodded a hello.

Gage, on the other hand, charmed the woman with a smile and a friendly greeting.

"Mr. and Mrs. Cooper," Ms. Lewitsky started. "Please relax, although I know this can be a bit nerve-racking. As Mr. Slater explained, today's meeting is just the start of the procedure. But I will warn you that we take the matter of issuing a green card through marriage very seriously. There are procedures in place for a reason, and there are no shortcuts. We scrutinize each application and make our decision only after we've spent time interviewing you, your family, and your friends." She shuffled some pieces of paper. "Everything seems to be in order here to commence the application. But tell me, Mrs. Cooper, how did the two of you meet?"

Charlotte took a deep breath. "We met through my work. I'm an environmental engineer, and the company I work for, Gold

Star Eco, works with oil companies to ensure their practices are compliant with environmental guidelines."

"It would be safe to say, Ms. Lewitsky," Gage interrupted smoothly, "that our initial interactions were a little heated. But when I met Charlotte in person for the first time"—he paused and looked over to her—"I knew I had to get to know her better."

Charlotte's breath hitched slightly. The look in his eyes was soft and, to a stranger, would seem loving. She had to give it to Gage, he was giving an Academy Award winning performance. It didn't seem forced—it seemed totally natural, almost like he really *did* love her, which was totally absurd, since it was all for the benefit of the interview.

If Gage could do it, she could do it, too. "Likewise for me, too, Ms. Lewitsky. Gage came thundering into my office to complain about something, I can't remember what now, but I knew, too, that I was done. There was no other man for me. Gage would be the man to own my future. " Her tongue tripped over the little white lie—she remembered exactly what he'd come complaining about: the land.

"Well, that's lovely," Ms. Lewitsky said. "It does look like you're suited. Now for a few more questions. You met through work. How long did you date before you decided to get married? And where did you go on your first date?"

First date?

Who asked a question like that, and why?

Oh shit, she and Gage hadn't even thought about questions like this. How the hell could they answer that? They hadn't dated at all, unless you called a picnic in a park a "date."

"Umm…" Hopefully Gage had an answer ready, but all he did was raise an eyebrow.

Typical male. When it came to the hard stuff, he walked away.

Fine, she could do this, and the best way would be to stick to as close to the truth as possible.

"Well," she started, "as we said, we had a few telephone calls that were business related and then Gage came to my office. That weekend I decided to take a trip to visit a town I'd been to a couple of times. It just so happens it was Gage's hometown, and he was visiting, too. I was eating at the local diner when the owner introduced me to Macy Young—you know, the famous country-and-western singer. Anyway, she is dating Gage's older brother and she invited me to go with her to the local bar. Since I didn't have any other plans, I said yes."

She paused and almost jumped when Gage's hand landed on hers. He squeezed it and continued where she left off.

"I can honestly say my mouth dropped open in surprise at seeing her there. We spent the night talking and we danced. It was a magical evening."

Again, Gage was giving a sterling performance of a man who was totally in love with his wife. It should've made her happy that he was doing such a convincing job, but it didn't. It was a lie.

And it hurt.

Deep down she wanted it to be true. She wanted Gage to love her.

A hand cupped her cheek. "Red?"

Gage's voice directed her attention back to the interview, away from the confusing thoughts swirling around her mind. "Sorry, I—" She needed to give a credible reason for her lapse in concentration. "I, uh, was remembering the song Macy sang that night. It was the same song we danced to on our wedding night as our first dance as a married couple."

Charlotte darted Ms. Lewitsky a look, hoping and praying that she was buying their story. Her face gave nothing away, and a ball of dread filled Charlotte's stomach.

God, she hoped they weren't going to get found out.

• • •

They walked out into the sunshine still holding hands. Charlotte wanted to rip her hand away from Gage's, but she couldn't as Ms. Lewitsky followed them out of the building.

Ms. Lewitsky held out her hand to both of them when they reached the sidewalk. "It was lovely meeting you, Mr. and Mrs. Cooper. I'll be in touch."

Both Gage and Charlotte shook her hand and she walked briskly down the street. Charlotte didn't let out the breath she had been holding until the woman disappeared around the corner.

"God, what a disaster," she said as she tried to pull her hand away from Gage's. His hand tightened, not letting hers go.

"Red, it wasn't a disaster at all. It was just the opposite. I think we totally convinced her that we married for love."

The *L* word. Who knew how four little letters could cause so much angst for people? Love was fabulous and remained that way for some. Or it started out fabulous before turning into a nightmare for others. Which was it going to be for her? She and Gage had to live together for at least the next two years, and while they sizzled up the sheets, she knew passion could fade. As for her, she'd fallen for the handsome Texan oilman—something she'd tried so hard not to do.

Yes. What she'd said to the immigration officer was one hundred percent true. Gage was it for her. She was done looking.

She hadn't realized Gage had stopped walking until he grabbed her arm. She turned to him, but his sunglasses hid his eyes, preventing her from seeing his thoughts.

"What?" she asked.

"I could ask you the same. Did you hear what I said about how we aced the interview?"

"It wasn't a school test. We didn't 'ace' anything. What we did, though, was portray a couple who, for all intents and purposes, convinced two other people we were in love. So yes, we totally fooled them." The bitterness of her words surprised her. She hadn't meant to sound that way, and she knew she'd offended Gage the minute he took a step back from her and released her hand.

"Isn't that what we were supposed to do?"

"Yes, but it didn't feel right. It felt dirty to lie to a government official."

The brightness of his smile dulled. "Right, well, I have another meeting to go to. Will you be okay getting back to your office?"

He was lying to her. He didn't really have a meeting. "I thought we were going to grab a cup of coffee after the meeting. When did this new meeting pop up?"

When he tugged on his tie, pulling the silky fabric through the collar, she knew her suspicions were correct.

Yes, she'd been bitchy in her comments. She owned that. But Gage didn't have to take so much offense that he would blow her off with a fake meeting. If that was how he wanted to play this game, then fine, she could play, as well.

"You know what? Don't bother trying to come up with a credible answer. I know you'd be lying. So go. Go back to your office, and I'll go back to mine."

Without waiting for a response, she turned on her heel and headed toward the cab that had conveniently pulled up a few feet in front of where they were standing. She got into the cab and gave the driver her office address. She looked out the window to see Gage standing on the curb, looking as dumbfounded as she herself felt.

• • •

Charlotte let herself into the condo after one of the worst days she'd had in a long while. After her fight with Gage, she'd returned to a mini–environmental crisis at the office. She'd spent the rest of the day sorting things out and working up a remedial plan for the beach that had been affected by a hazmat leak.

The only good thing about the crisis was that it helped her keep her mind off Gage.

Silence greeted her as she closed the front door behind her. Oil Slick didn't even come running like she normally did the moment Charlotte arrived home. Where was the cat? She knew Gage hadn't taken Oil Slick to work, because of the meeting they'd had with the immigration officer.

God, when did it matter where the damn cat was? The animal wasn't her responsibility. She tossed her keys into the bowl on the hallway table and dumped her laptop bag underneath the same table.

She released her hair from its businesslike bun. Her fingers massaged her sore scalp where the pins had begun to dig into it. Gage hadn't told her he wouldn't be home, but then again she hadn't waited for him to collect her from the office like she normally did.

What a mess the day had been—a day she'd rather forget.

She walked into the master suite, slipped off her shoes, and tossed her handbag onto the bed. It would be so easy just to crawl under the covers and forget the whole day had ever happened.

But what she needed to do was get their marriage certificate before she forgot. Her office wanted a copy of it for their records, but she had no idea where it was. She assumed it would be in Gage's study.

Leaving the master bedroom, she walked down the hall to Gage's office. She had only been in this room a few times, once to distract Gage while he worked late at night. Even while still annoyed at him, she couldn't stop the smile, when memories of what they'd gotten up to in the room filled her mind. They certainly didn't have any issues when it came to sex.

Flicking on the light, she wandered over to the desk and sat in his chair. Now, where would their marriage certificate most likely be? She started with the desk drawers but she came up empty handed. Next, she pulled the tray that had a neat stack of papers in it toward her.

She picked up the first piece of paper and scanned it.

No, it couldn't be. Could it? He wouldn't do that to her—surely. She reread the subject line and the body of the e-mail.

Survey Report: 12332 Pine Ramble Drive, Sweet Ridge, TX

Dear Gage,

Thanks for the opportunity to provide you with a survey report of the abovementioned property.

At your request, we conducted a preliminary survey of the land and surrounding areas. Attached is the report of our findings.

If you have any questions with regard to the report, please do not hesitate to contact us.

Yours sincerely,

Bubba Fredricks

The son of a bitch. He'd let her talk night after night about what she'd do to the house, the renovations she'd make in the future. He'd even made his own suggestions about what they could do to the house. He had her believing he actually cared about the land.

And it was all a game to suck her into thinking he gave a damn, that her ideas mattered. His word was worth nothing when stacked against the almighty dollar he could make from the oil. She couldn't believe Gage had gone back on his promise to her.

Where was the report? She knew Gage had to have printed it out. There was no way he wouldn't have. She knew how much that piece of land meant to him. The evidence of the e-mail in her hand was proof of how much he wanted what lay beneath the surface of sand and rocks.

She picked up a stack of papers from the pile in the tray and flipped through the neatly stapled groups. Sure enough, there was the report. Putting the rest of the papers back into the tray, she started to read the document.

As she scanned the report, she was stunned when she read exactly what had been found on her land—a huge oil pocket that would prove very profitable for Gage. Pity he would never get his hands on the land now. They had no written agreement about her selling it to him. And right now she didn't even care about her green card.

She'd trusted Gage. She'd fallen in love with him. She'd started to think he was beginning to care for her, as well. He had betrayed her. All his touches and caring words had been an act. Just like today in front of the immigration official—he *did* deserve an Academy Award, because he'd had her convinced they could have a future together.

Charlotte sat back in the chair and considered her options. She had a job, albeit a temporary one. Once her contract ended, she would go back to Australia and find another job. There was no point in thinking her future was in Houston and Sweet Ridge. She couldn't decide what to do with the land right now. That could wait—it wasn't going anywhere.

But she was. She couldn't stay in this condo anymore. She could go back to her old apartment. The company had paid for the lease for the length of her stay. But she didn't want to go back there, either. That would probably be the first place Gage would look for her.

She had to make a decision—and quickly. Gage could walk through the door at any minute, and she didn't want to be here when he arrived home. She would pack a bag and just go to a hotel for a few nights. Once Gage worked out that whatever they'd had together was finished, she'd move back to her apartment. In all likelihood, the thought of not getting the oil he so coveted would be more upsetting than her leaving him.

Decision made, she reached for a blank piece of paper and wrote a note. She placed it in the middle of his desk. Right on top of the report. There was no way he could miss it.

Chapter 24

Gage was flying high as he rode the elevator to his condo. The cat followed. Who knew Oil Slick would be the key to finalizing one of the biggest deals his company had negotiated? With this new deal and the prospect of mining Dad's land, his company would be able to ride out the next slump in the oil industry. Hopefully by the time he'd got the various permits required, civil work contracts negotiated and set up drilling contractors the price of oil would've stabilized.

He couldn't wait to celebrate this new deal with Charlotte and talk to her about the survey report he'd received. He knew he would need to do some smooth talking, as he'd promised he wouldn't survey the land until after their marriage was over. But what woman wouldn't be happy with the prospect of becoming very wealthy—and that's what mining the land would give to Charlotte. She'd not only have her green card, but she'd have more money than she would be able to spend in her lifetime. Money might not seem important to her now. But when she saw her bank account with all those zeroes, she wouldn't be able to resist the new lifestyle it would give her.

"We've got this, Oil Slick," he murmured to the cat while opening his front door. Then he called out, "Red? I'm home. Sorry I'm late."

He stopped two feet in the door. The apartment was dark. Like it had been when he lived by himself. Since Charlotte had moved in, she always had on nearly all the lights in the place. He knew he was late, but not so late that she wouldn't already be home from work.

A ball of dread began to grow inside of him. Had something happened to her? With quick, efficient movements he set Oil Slick free and then reached for his phone. No missed calls. No waiting text messages. And no unread e-mails from Charlotte.

Where could she be?

Gage pulled up his "favorites" in his contact list and hit Charlotte's name. Her phone immediately went to voice mail.

"Hey, Red, it's me. I'm home and you're not here. Are you okay? Call me when you get this message. I've got some great news."

He clicked off and slipped his phone back into his pocket. Gage hadn't contacted her during the day, because he had to admit, he had still been a bit annoyed about their argument after they'd left the lawyer's office. It had been a stupid fight, and he still didn't even know how it started. He should've chased after her instead of letting her walk away from him in anger.

But he didn't want to let her know he was falling for her. He'd answered the questions in the lawyer's office honestly. There was no acting or lying on his part. He loved knowing that he would come home and find her here, waiting for him. Or that she'd meet him downstairs at her own work office, and they'd go home together. He liked sharing his day with her. The fact that she worked in the same industry as him was more than he could ask for. They understood each other all the more because of that.

Gage started his search for Charlotte in their bedroom. He chuckled softly—since when had his master bedroom become 'their bedroom'? The answer was easy—the moment she moved in.

Empty.

He headed down the hallway to check out the spare room.

Empty.

He walked through the apartment. There was no sign of her. For some reason she wasn't home. The ball of dread grew even bigger.

The last room he went into was his study. On occasion she'd curl up in a chair with a book while he dealt with e-mails. He didn't expect her to be there, but he'd check it out anyway.

The moment he walked in, he knew Charlotte had been in the room. His desk was normally clear of papers. But tonight, sitting in the middle of the shiny wood was a piece of paper. The cat brushed up against his leg as he stood looking at the top of his desk. He didn't know why he was reluctant to go and pick it up. Everything in him told him who wrote the note. And it wasn't from his housekeeper, who'd been there earlier.

"Damn it, cat." He stooped and picked up the creature before she used his leg as a scratching post again. Gage went over to his desk and picked up the paper.

Gage,

I'm leaving you. I don't appreciate being lied to, and the report I found on your desk shows me just how much that piece of land means to you. Maybe Jack knew something when he left it to me instead of you. I can't believe you went behind my back and arranged a survey of the land. You broke your promise. How many more will you break?

Anyway, it doesn't matter. I will be going back to Australia when my work contract ends. I have no reason to get a green card now. I can't stay married to a man who lies to me. And I can't pretend for the next two years just to get a piece of paper.

I hope the report keeps you warm at night, because that's the closest you're going to get to the oil you so covet. I will never sell the land to you now.

Charlotte

He reread the note a dozen times. Each time the hurt in her words stabbed deeper inside of him.

"I fucked up big-time, Oil Slick."

The cat jumped off his lap and stalked away, as if disgusted with what he'd done, as well.

He couldn't blame Charlotte for feeling like she'd been played. He hadn't been thinking about anyone but himself when he went ahead and ordered the report. He *knew* he was going back on his word, and yet he still did it. Even as he walked through the door tonight, he'd thought he could sweet-talk her into forgiving him.

He'd disappointed yet another person in his life. Maybe Grayson was right when he'd accused him of still doing things without thinking of the consequences. This time it was Charlotte he'd disappointed, the one person who meant as much to him as his dad had meant. How could he have done that to her?

If the tables had been turned and she'd betrayed him like this, he'd be steaming mad, too. He had to find her and apologize. He didn't know how to make it up to her, but he would.

He knew exactly where she'd be. Before the night was over, she'd be back in this house where she belonged.

• • •

Three hours later Gage walked through his front door again, dejected and frustrated. He'd driven to her apartment and knocked on her door. When he got no response, he went down and waited in the foyer. But the longer he waited, the more obvious it became she wasn't returning there.

Calling the hotels in the vicinity of his condo, her old apartment, and her office wasn't a feasible option. There were too many of them. And he doubted any hotel would divulge guest information, no matter how sweetly he asked.

The next option would be to go to Gold Star Eco tomorrow and see her there. He would insist on taking her out to lunch so they could talk in private without everyone in her office overhearing their conversation.

The silence of the apartment closed in on him. It hadn't bothered him before, but tonight he missed Charlotte. He missed her quiet presence beside him, missed her joking with him over dinner. He even missed her scolding Oil Slick for scratching at the couch. He just plain missed her.

The box of letters still sat in the middle of the coffee table, the gold key sticking out of the lock. What happiness had he found since he'd discovered the letters? He hadn't found any happiness in reading them, but he hadn't read them all. Maybe it was time to man up. Perhaps something in his father's words would help him to work out how to apologize to Charlotte.

He reached out and grabbed the box, placing it on the couch next to him. Unlocking it, he lifted the lid and pulled out the small bundle. He placed the ones he'd already read back in the box. Taking a deep breath, he picked up the next one in the pile.

An hour later he picked up the last letter, his heart heavy. Through the letters he'd discovered that Dad and Nora's relationship had started to fall apart. Although with no dates to go by, Gage had no idea how whether their relationship lasted for two years or six months. She'd stopped responding to his letters. But Jack had kept writing, holding out hope that she would respond. His father hadn't elaborated on what he'd done wrong, and it frustrated Gage. Then again, why would Dad write about what he'd done wrong to the woman who already knew?

This final letter was a couple of pages long, longer than any letter either one of them had written to each other.

My darling, sweet Nora,

My heart is broken, and I don't think it will ever be fully healed. Finding all the letters I'd written to you when I went to check the box today … well, all I can say is I fell to my knees and cried. You will probably never read this one last letter because I have the box with me, but I have to write it. Closure, it could be called perhaps. I don't know.

The fact that you hadn't burned the letters I sent you gave me a little bit of hope that you might forgive me, but I saw you leave town today. I don't know how long you're going for. You may already be back, or you may never return. Seeing you in that car, laughing with someone other than me as it drove away, told me all I needed to know. You haven't laughed like that with me for a while.

I will never love another like I love you, Nora. You are the one who makes my world whole. I could spend the rest of my life a bachelor, or I may find another woman to care for. But I won't love her as much as I love you. I can't when I've had a love so fulfilling as the one I shared with you. I know my love for you will never die. It will always be an ache inside of me. I admit that I'm vain enough to want children, someone to pass my legacy on to. I wish we could've had them together. You would make a wonderful mother.

I'm sorry that I got so caught up with the future I envisioned for us that I forgot to include you, to ask if you shared the same dream. It will always be my biggest regret. I wish you would've given me a chance to explain. I don't know why you didn't. I'd have slowed down in my planning—all you had to do was ask. Or maybe I should've known you were scared. I know I also got caught up in making a success of my business. Again, I was working so hard for us—for you. It was all for you. I will never live in the house I purchased for us. It would hurt too much to spend any time there. But I can't part with it, either. Call me stupid or sentimental, but I'll keep it and hope and pray that one day you'll come back to me. If not, then I know I will find someone who will love and appreciate it as much as I do. That house connects me to you.

I wish I could change things. But I can't and I must live with my actions. I must live with the knowledge that it was through my hand, my selfishness to prove to you that I can give you everything you want, that I destroyed what was given freely to me: Your love. Your light. Your smile. Just know that I hope one day I will be able to give you this letter and show you that nothing is more important to me than you and your happiness.

I love you, Nora, for all eternity.

Your Jack

The last page of the letter slipped through his fingers, his own heart hurting at the pain in every word that Dad had written. He leaned back against the cushions of the couch and closed his eyes.

He wished Charlotte was here beside him. He wished he could share this last letter with her. He wished he could've shared all the letters with her. The romance between Dad and this Nora was beautiful and fulfilling, just like his father had said. But even Gage could see from the pleading in the words Nora wrote that she was struggling with Jack's passion for work and his actions toward her. She didn't say it in so many words, and maybe Gage could see it better because he was an outsider.

But why was Nora so unsure of her place in Jack's life?

He picked up the letter again. He knew Dad was sending him a message, and as he read the second to last line again, he knew what his father meant. For so long Gage had coveted the land—the land Dad had bought for the love of his life. Dad would never have mined it. It was supposed to have been his family's home. And he'd kept the house clean and well-maintained in the hope that one day Nora would return. Then Jack placed the letters in the box he had made in the one place he knew they'd be safe.

Always hoping that Nora would come back to him.

Dad had finally given up the hope of a future of happiness on that land. And then Dad had met Charlotte. He'd seen a light in her and had known she would love the land like he had. Had Dad also seen something in Charlotte that he'd known would attract Gage? Had Dad played matchmaker in his last months on earth?

Just thinking about Charlotte caused his heart to ache. Was this how Dad had felt when he saw Nora riding away in a stranger's car? Gage knew that if he saw Charlotte driving away like that, he wouldn't be able to go on.

In that instant he knew. He knew with everything in him.

He loved her.

He loved Charlotte with the same intensity that Dad had loved Nora. Deep inside of him, Gage knew that if somehow Charlotte changed her mind and gave him the land, he wouldn't be able to mine it. The two visits they'd spent at the house had been times he would cherish.

Hadn't he even imagined a future there with her? A future with their kids. A future where he and his brothers grilled out while their kids played together. And Dad, that wily old bastard, had worked out that Gage needed a woman who would turn his focus from business to love. That was exactly what Charlotte had done. Over the time they'd been living together, he'd found himself becoming less intense about needing to prove himself.

He suspected that, like Dad, he was a one-woman man—and that Charlotte was that woman for him.

The key to everything is happiness.

Yes, he'd been happier than ever with Charlotte in his life, and some of their best times had been at the house in Sweet Ridge. The house Dad had bought for his love—Nora.

He gazed around his stark, soulless apartment. This wasn't his home. His home was with Charlotte, and he knew exactly how he could show her that she was first in his life, not the black gold that lived under layers of rocks and soil he'd coveted for so long. From now on, he was going to covet Charlotte. Like the line in Dad's letter, nothing was more important to him than Charlotte and her happiness.

He just had to win her back.

Chapter 25

Charlotte dumped her laptop bag on her desk. All she wanted to do was go to the hotel, collapse in a heap, and sleep until she couldn't sleep anymore. But she knew she would have a million things to catch up on in the office. And judging by the pile of papers in her in-tray, she would be here till midnight.

The day after she'd walked out on Gage, she'd been sent out to the site that had the spill the day of their interview with the immigration officer. The problems had kept coming, so she'd ended up staying a week and a half. And not once had Gage tried to contact her except for one call the night she'd walked out. She had cried herself to sleep that night. The bed had seemed so big and lonely without Gage.

After the third day with no contact from Gage, she didn't need to be hit over the head with a sledgehammer to know that what they'd shared was over. She had thought he'd at least try more than once to call her. She supposed now that she was back, she would need to contact the immigration lawyer and halt the process for the green card. And she would have to look at flights back to Australia. But before all of that, she had to get through today. The weekend loomed in a few hours. At least last weekend she had been out of town, so she'd had her work to help keep her mind off Gage.

Charlotte yawned again. Sleep had been as elusive as the pot of gold at the end of a rainbow. She picked up the top item in her tray: a report about an ecological study of a tract of land and the impact that drilling said land would have on the natural flora and fauna inhabiting it.

The words blurred in front of her. It was hopeless. She wouldn't be able to concentrate on anything and be useful without sleep.

She'd take a few reports home with her and read them over the weekend.

"Oh, hey, Charlotte, I didn't realize you'd returned." Meredith stood in the doorway of her office.

"I just got in, but I think I might head home. I'm exhausted—it's been a long week and half."

"Yeah, I saw some of the e-mails you sent at all hours of the morning. I don't think the boss will mind you leaving early, especially since it's Friday. And I bet you're anxious to see that yummy husband of yours."

Charlotte fought to keep the smile on her face. Having to tell everyone in the office that her marriage was over wasn't something she really wanted to do just yet—although it would have to be said soon. She hated having to tell Allen she no longer planned to stay in the States so she couldn't stay with the company. There went her chance to get a good work recommendation from him.

"Yes, I am anxious to get home," she responded, a noncommittal answer at best. "Was there something you wanted, Meredith?"

The sooner Meredith left, the sooner she could get back home—no, to *the hotel.* Charlotte didn't have a home anymore.

"Oh yes, this parcel arrived the other day, and for some reason I forgot to put it on your desk. I was just coming to do it when I saw you here."

"Thanks." She held out her hand for it. "I think I'll take this and leave now."

"Have a good weekend, Charlotte." Meredith waved as she backed out of her office.

Charlotte studied the parcel. It was wrapped in plain brown paper, giving her no idea who sent it, as there was no return address. Whatever was in the box was light. Even though the temptation to open it was strong, she wanted to wait until she could guarantee she wouldn't get interrupted.

Setting the box back down on her desk, she picked up the pile of mail and took a quick look through it. Nothing was terribly urgent, so it could all wait until she returned to the office on Monday.

Collecting all her belongings and the box, she headed out the office door, wishing that instead of a lonely hotel room, she was heading home to Gage's welcoming arms.

• • •

The shower revived her so she felt a little more like herself. Charlotte finished blow-drying her hair and walked out of the bathroom. The parcel sat in the middle of one of the double beds in the room. Now she could open it.

She wrestled with the tape. Whoever had wrapped it had done a great job. Giving up on using her fingernails after another one broke, she opened her suitcase and pulled out the small pocketknife she always traveled with. Finally, the tape gave and she was able to get a grip on the paper. She peeled back the layers until she found a rectangular-shaped wooden box. It immediately reminded her of the box Gage had found filled with Jack's letters. Tears filled her eyes.

Had he read any more of his father's letters? She dashed away the tears and any thoughts of Gage. What they had was over.

Inside the box she found a small key. Was this some kind of joke? She shuffled through the papers until she found an envelope with her name scrawled across the front of it.

Gage's handwriting.

Her heart skipped a beat at the symbolic nature of the parcel she'd been sent. Opening the envelope, she pulled out the piece of paper.

My darling, sweet Texas fire,

I'm hoping that you are reading this and haven't torn it up when you worked out the parcel was from me.

I have a request and I hope you won't deny me. Even though I know I don't deserve it, I hope you will agree to my request so that I can explain. I have so much I want to say to you, Red. So very much.

I will be down at Sweet Ridge this weekend and every weekend for the rest of my life, waiting and hoping that one day you will come and visit. I will be parked in the driveway of your house (I hope you won't sell it) at 11 a.m. every Saturday until I'm unable to visit it anymore.

Until Saturday…

Love,

Gage

Charlotte folded the notecard, and the light caught the diamond of her engagement ring. She hadn't taken the rings off. She touched the diamond. The rings were so gorgeous and so expensive, more than a marriage that was only a "business arrangement" had really deserved. A marriage based on love deserved the rings that adorned her finger.

She looked at the key and the note. Did she have the courage to go and see him, to hear what he had to say? Could she even trust what he had to say? Had her leaving awakened him to the fact that he didn't get everything he wanted with a smile and a healthy bank account? Would he even follow through on his declaration and go to the house every weekend? She immediately squashed that thought. While he'd gone back on his word about the survey, she didn't think he'd go back on this. He'd sent her a note. A handwritten note with a key—exactly like what Jack had left him when he'd died. And Jack had written notes to his Nora. Yes, Gage would wait every Saturday for the rest of his life down at Sweet Ridge.

Charlotte couldn't let him do that. Even if she didn't really want to hear what he had to say, he did deserve to a chance to explain.

Plus, she loved him. Her heart hurt thinking of a future without him in it. She could admit she'd let her temper get the better of her that night at the condo. She should've waited so he could explain what he'd done. But the hurt at the thought he was playing with her had made rational thinking go out the window.

Decision made, she packed an overnight bag. She would leave tonight and spend the weekend at Sweet Ridge to hear what Gage had to say. And then she'd make a final decision about her future.

• • •

Saturday morning dawned, and restless energy had Charlotte up with the sparrows. She went for a quick run, avoiding the main street so she wasn't tempted to go into Betty Lou's Diner. She'd even picked up takeout on the drive down the previous night so she wouldn't be seen around town. She hid in her hotel room, and, maybe because she knew she was going to see Gage, she slept better than she had in a while.

Now the time had come to head toward the house. She picked up the box with the key and put it into her large tote. Butterflies had migrated to her belly and decided to have a party.

She took a deep breath as she got into her car and started it. The drive would take her about thirty-five minutes. Thirty-five minutes during which she hoped her nerves wouldn't cause her to pull over and throw up what little breakfast she'd managed to eat after her run. Not even when she and Gage had stood in front of Phil waiting for him to marry them had she felt this nervous. That was the time to feel sick with nerves, not now.

She turned on the radio, and Macy's sweet voice filled the inside of her car. Fate was playing with her as she recognized the song as the one that she and Gage had danced to twice: once at the Silver Spurs the first time she'd been at Sweet Ridge with him, and the second on their wedding night. This really and truly was "their song".

Before she knew it, she was turning into the driveway of the house. The surface seemed smoother than it had the last time she'd traveled it. As the house came into view, she gasped in surprise.

"What the hell?" The house had been painted. Flowerpots with brightly colored blooms adorned either side of the steps leading up the porch to the front door. The closer she got, she also saw that the garden beds had been tidied up and new plants filled the freshly churned soil.

Something was missing, though. Gage's car wasn't in the driveway, and the garage stood open. That was empty, too. Charlotte looked at the clock in the car. It showed five minutes after eleven. Her heart plummeted to the soles of her feet. So much for him being here every Saturday.

She parked her car and grabbed her tote bag. The smell of fresh paint still lingered in the air. She had to admit the house looked sparkling bright with the fresh coat of paint.

As she reached the front door, the realization struck that she'd forgotten her key. She slapped her palm against her forehead. How could she have been so silly? She now remembered putting the key in her bedside drawer the day they'd returned from the last trip she and Gage had taken.

But she did have another key, didn't she? Reaching into her tote bag, she pulled out the box Gage had sent and opened it. The shiny metal winked up at her. It looked too new to belong to this house, but it was all she had. Plucking it from its velvety cushion, she inserted it into the door lock and turned. It gave easily, and breathing deeply, she opened the wooden door.

Multiple scents and sights assailed her when she walked in. Her tote slipped off her shoulder and landed on the floor.

Her previously partially empty house now appeared to be fully furnished. The wooden staircase gleamed with furniture polish. The living room looked exactly how she'd envisioned it that first night she'd spent together with Gage, sharing her dreams of the house while cuddled with him on the air mattress.

Charlotte walked through to the kitchen, tears filling her eyes. Again, it was exactly as she'd wanted the kitchen to be. The cupboard doors looked brand-new with their new stain. The walls were a light but fresh yellow. The wall she'd talked about demolishing had been torn down, creating the open-plan layout she'd hoped it would.

"It's perfect," she whispered.

"Hello, Red. I was hoping you'd come."

Charlotte whirled around and stopped herself from rushing into Gage's arms. He stood not three feet away from her, Oil Slick in his arms. She smiled when she caught sight of the bright pink ribbon around the cat's neck as it squirmed to be let down. Gage obliged its request and Oil Slick scampered over to her. She bent down and picked her up, burying her face into the soft fur. Charlotte needed a few moments to get her feelings under control, and Oil Slick provided her with the perfect excuse.

When she felt she had her emotions in check, she put the cat on the ground and faced Gage. He looked tired. His hair was mussed, but he was clean-shaven and smelled divine.

"Hello, Gage."

They stood there in the center of the kitchen for a few awkward moments. Eventually Gage closed the distance between them.

"I—uh..." He ran a hand down his face. Clearly he was nervous, too. "I'm sorry."

She opened her mouth to speak when he held up his hand to halt her words.

"No, don't speak. Not until you hear me out. Can you do that, please?"

She nodded.

"Good," he responded before he grabbed her hand and led her through to the living room. Her skin sizzled beneath his fingers. Her body craved his touch. She had missed it desperately while she'd been away.

They sat down on the couch, and that was when Charlotte saw the box containing Jack's letters.

"Did you read them?" she asked.

The corner of Gage's mouth quirked up. "I thought I told you to hear me out before you spoke."

She rolled her eyes at him. The teasing eased the tension between them. "Sorry."

He nodded and traced a line down her left hand until his finger connected with her wedding and engagement rings. "I should've known my feelings for you were more complex than I thought when I picked out these rings. I'd gone into the jewelry store, prepared to get you just a plain gold wedding band. No engagement ring. Nothing flashy. It was just a business arrangement, wasn't it?

"But then I saw this set, and nothing else would do for my Red. I didn't give it a second thought when I bought them." He lifted her hand and kissed the rings softly. Her breath stuttered at the look in his eyes. It gave her hope.

"I know I don't deserve you. I've done everything wrong from the beginning. I was so arrogant to think I could talk my way out of what I'd done, ordering the survey when I said I wouldn't. Even when I sent the e-mail, I knew it was wrong, but all I could think about was the oil on this land. How much I'd always wanted it. How much I resented Dad for not giving it to me. Out of all the things I've done since I met you, arranging for that survey is the one thing I wish I could change."

"Why did you do it?" she asked, even though he had tried to explain his reasoning. "Why didn't you send another e-mail canceling the request?"

"I don't know. I felt like Dad was still punishing me for the stupid mistake I made in college, for how that mistake crushed the dreams he'd had for me."

"I hardly think Jack was punishing you for something that happened so long ago. What did you do that was so bad?"

A look of self-derision crossed his face. "I thought I was untouchable in college. I was so arrogant, even then. I didn't think the rules applied to me. How could they? I was the star running back of the football team. I was on the road to winning the Heisman Trophy in my freshman year. We were going to win the championship that year—because of me."

He paused and Charlotte realized how much it was costing him to tell her what he'd done. She squeezed his hand tighter. No matter what he told her, she wasn't going to stop loving him.

She smiled, encouraging him to continue.

"I'd been pushing the boundaries and rules for weeks. The guys on the team got me into their fraternity. I didn't have to do half the stuff the other candidates had to do to be initiated. I thought those guys were my friends. I was so stupid back then."

Charlotte had a fair idea where this story was headed, and it wasn't a happy ending.

"Turns out the ringleader, a fellow running back, was jealous. He'd been the star of the team until I arrived. My stats left his in the dust. His end goal was to get me kicked off the team. So he got his friends to help him achieve that goal. They really didn't have to do too much to encourage me to break the rules. As I said, I thought I was untouchable. Turns out I wasn't. I got busted doing one fraternity prank too many. That, along with all the warnings and reprimands I'd gotten for being late to practice, for getting caught in Vegas for underage gambling, and for letting my grades fall, was all the athletic director needed. I got kicked off the team, and because I was there on a full scholarship, I got kicked out of school, too. All the dreams Dad had of me getting drafted into the NFL went up in smoke."

"Oh, Gage, couldn't you have tried to appeal the decision or go to another school? Surely another college would've been champing at the bit to get you on their team."

He shrugged. "I suppose I could've, but I was so ashamed. Also, once you get a reputation for being a rule breaker, no one really wants to touch you in case you tarnish the reputation of their school. It was a wake-up call for me. I ended up heading back to Houston and found a job on an oil rig. I kept any contact with Dad and my brothers to a minimum. I knew I'd disappointed them. I wanted to prove to them I wasn't a deadbeat. So I worked on the rigs and got my degree though an online college—and here I am today."

"You should be proud of all you've achieved. Not everyone would go on to be so successful. Some people would've found solace in alcohol or drugs."

He laughed sardonically. "You'd think so, but I haven't learned, have I? I disappointed you the same way I disappointed the rest of my family."

Charlotte opened her mouth to refute his claims. He placed two fingers over her lips.

"No, don't say I didn't disappoint you, because I know it's not true." He looked deep into her eyes, remorse shining in the depths of his own. "I always thought mining this land would redeem myself in Dad's eyes. The royalties from the oil here would've provided him with more money than he would have known what to do with. And his screw-up of a son would have given it to him. But he died before I could show him I was worthy to call myself the youngest son of Jack Cooper."

Charlotte shook her head. His reasoning seemed silly to her, but to Gage, it meant a lot. "I think you underestimated Jack. He might not have mentioned your name to me, but he talked about all of his boys and how proud he was of all they'd achieved so far in their lives." She paused for a moment. "But if you desperately want to drill here on this land, then why did you do all of this to the house? Why make it into my dream home?"

"I've done some thinking while we were apart. I read all of Dad's letters. I now know why he left you this house and land."

"You do? There was something in the letters? Or had he written you a letter?"

"Yes, there was something in the letters. Dad left you this land because he knew you would love it and treasure it like he did. Whether he had insight into the future or he was reaching for the stars, I don't really know. But he knew you were the one person who could make me see there was more to life than drilling the next oil well.

"And he was right." She closed her eyes as he brushed a hand down her face. "Oh, how he was right, Red. The first weekend, when you laid in my arms and shared your vision for the house, I could see it. I wanted to be the man whom you came down here with. I wanted to be the man who walked with you along the beach. I wanted to be the man who pushed our kids on the swing set. I want all that now—with you, Charlotte Cooper."

The sincerity in his words couldn't be denied, and the tears that had filled her eyes when she entered the house returned and spilled down her cheeks.

"I don't know what to say, Cowboy."

"Say you want it, too. Say you love me like I love you. And I do love you, Charlotte. So much. Not talking to you this last week and a half has been hell. I wanted to storm into your office the day after you left and just carry you out. But then I knew what I had to do. I had to make you see that *you* are the most important thing to me—your dreams. Making them come true is worth more to me than the oil in the ground here. This house was supposed to be Dad's home with his one true love. Maybe it can be *our* home—together. Maybe we can fulfill the dream that eluded Dad and Nora."

She was still reeling with Gage's declaration of love to fully comprehend his statement about the house.

"Why didn't he live here with your mum?"

Gage smiled softly. "Simple, really. He bought this house for Nora, and when she broke up with him, he was so heartbroken that he couldn't stand to live here without her. I don't think he loved my mom like he loved Nora. I'm sure he loved her in his own way, though, just not the same way. And I can't deny he loved us boys. We were his future. He was always there at our games, cheering us on. I like to think that maybe there was something in you that reminded him of his Nora. That was why he left the house to you. He knew you would love it like he did, and he was right."

Her eyes widened when Gage moved off the couch and got down on one knee. He picked up her left hand and pulled off her engagement ring. He brought it to his mouth and gave it a kiss before he looked into her eyes.

"What are you doing?"

"I cheated you out of a proper proposal. I need to make it right. Charlotte Wilkinson, you lit a fire in me the day I walked into your office. I didn't know it then, but I know it now. You own my heart. I love you and I hope that one day you can love me, too." He slipped the ring on her finger. "Will you do me the honor of marrying me?"

Charlotte swallowed on the ball of emotion in her throat at the enormity of the gesture. She wasn't a hearts-and-flowers type of girl and hadn't given the way Gage proposed a thought. The fact he had proved how much she meant to him. The need to be close to Gage overwhelmed her, and she climbed off the couch and wrapped her arms around his neck. "Yes," she whispered. "So much yes. I'd be thrilled to marry you and be your wife. And that day is here, Cowboy. I love you so much that the thought of leaving Texas and never seeing you again almost crippled me. I knew I couldn't stay here in the States if I didn't have you in my life. I definitely knew I couldn't visit this house again." She kissed his lips briefly before pulling back. "I love you, Gage Cooper. Every single flawed part of you. I can't believe you've made my dreams come true with this house."

"Red, I want to make all your dreams come true. Maybe in a few years we can move down here permanently."

"I'd love that. Until then we can come every weekend."

Gage's answer was to capture her lips. She melted into his kiss. It was a kiss of apology and hope for a new life together. She answered back, agreeing with him, letting him know she trusted and believed in him.

He broke away from her and lifted her chin so she was looking directly at him. The love shining out of his eyes warmed her completely.

"I finally understand the meaning of Dad's note to me."

"And what's that?"

"His note said, '*The key to everything is happiness.*' He wanted me to read those letters to know that *love* is the key to everything, not only material things. Maybe he was playing matchmaker, I don't know, but *you* are my key, my love, my happiness. You are my everything."

She smiled through her tears. "And you are mine."

Acknowledgments

To my fellow authors in crime, Robyn Neeley and Monica Tillery — I love working with you girls. This series has been so much fun to write. Robyn, thanks for sharing your great idea with us.

Tara, Julie, and the Crimson team — it's always a pleasure to work with you all. Thanks for liking this concept and helping us shape it into the series it is.

Jennifer, all your hard work on teasers, tweets, and Facebook posts is appreciated so much. Enjoy working with you, girl.

To all my readers— honestly, I know I say it in every book, but thank you for taking the time to pick up my books, read them, and leave reviews I'm so grateful for each and every one of you.

To the loves of my life, Jason, Princess, and Sports Dude— I know I drive you crazy with being on the computer all the time, but I couldn't do this without you.

More from This Author
Tangled Vines
by Nicole Flockton

Laughter filtered through Kyle Davis's closed door. He gave the New York stock market one last look, then shut down his computer. He would have to join the crowd.

With precise movements, he put his laptop in his bag and walked the short distance to his door. A loud chorus of "We Wish You a Merry Christmas" greeted him as he opened it with a forced smile. Kyle didn't mind going to any other office party the firm put on. Except this one—the annual Christmas party. If he could sneak out, he would. Unfortunately, his obligation as owner of the company forced him to attend.

"You okay, Kyle?" This voice he recognized. He'd heard it in all forms. Angry. Happy. Sad. Annoyed.

Smiling down at his assistant, he touched her arm briefly before putting his hand in his pants pocket. "Yes, Shey, I'm fine."

"Thanks for hanging around. I know it's hard."

"Yes, you do." He quirked his eyebrow at her. "Yet you continually arrange for this event to be held on the night I leave."

Shey placed her hands on her hips. "That's because this is your firm, Kyle. You have a responsibility to be here." A waiter passed by carrying a tray full of drinks. She plucked a bottle of beer off the tray and handed it to him. "Now drink and be happy."

Kyle took the cool bottle and brought it to his lips. He took a couple of swallows, welcoming the bitter taste of the beer. "Why do you always organize the party to be held in the office? Why not at a restaurant or private room at a club?"

“Because if I did that, you wouldn’t turn up. At least here, outside your office, you have no choice but to attend.”

“I might have to arrange for an interior designer to come in next year and change the layout of the office. I’ll make my office as far away as possible from everyone,” he grumbled.

Shey laughed and lightly punched him on his arm. “You wouldn’t. Any other time of the year you like to look out and see everyone working. The king surveying his kingdom.” She paused and took a sip of her own beer. “It’s only this time of year you act like a bear with a sore head.”

“I should fire you.”

“Not the first time you’ve said that. I imagine it won’t be the last. It’s lucky I know and love you.”

Kyle leaned down and kissed her cheek. “I know.” He lowered his voice so only Shey could hear what he had to say next. “Thanks, Shey. For being you.”

Twenty minutes later, after his obligatory thank-you-for-your-hard-work speech, he headed toward the door. The people who had been working with him for a few years knew his habit of cutting out early. They never questioned him. They knew better. His staff liked their jobs too much. He paid them handsomely for their loyalty.

“Kyle, wait.”

He stopped and glanced over his shoulder at Shey. “Yes?”

“Have a nice holiday.” She winked before she turned and headed back to the party.

The noise from the party faded as he made his way toward the bank of elevators. He glanced at his watch—it was close to ten p.m. The sensible part of him said he should wait until morning to set off for his Margaret River house. He ignored it. The car was packed. At this time of the evening traffic would be light. There would be no snarls slowing down his journey.

Solitude beckoned. He would answer her call.

• • •

Kyle inserted the key into the door that led from the garage into his kitchen. He placed his case on the ground, stretching his arms above his neck to loosen his tight muscles. The silence shrouded him. He welcomed the feeling of calm that always washed over him when he walked into this house.

He'd bought it a year ago from a couple no longer able to maintain the residence plus the ten acres of land surrounding it. He'd managed a few weekend trips during the year to enjoy the house and the Margaret River surf. But he had to admit he hadn't managed a trip here for the last couple of months. While the house had been renovated in recent times, the vines and fruit trees had been neglected. The garden was a total mess. He'd hired a caretaker to look after the house when he wasn't there and to do basic maintenance on the trees and vines. He had to make some decisions soon about what he was going to do with the area. Ripping it out and putting in a pool and pool house seemed a good option.

He clamped down on thoughts about property maintenance. He was here to forget it was Christmas. He'd deal with the garden in the New Year when Ted, his caretaker, was back from sick and annual leave and Kyle had his mind firmly focused on the present. Not on the past.

Kyle wandered through the house with the familiarity of someone who always walked through it in the dark.

He stripped off his shirt and made his way to the French doors overlooking the back of his property. The moon cast a bright white glow over the yard. He blinked and then blinked again. He reached over to the wall and flipped the switch. Light flooded the outside of his house.

"What the hell?" Where once slightly overgrown rows of vines resided, now sleek, straight rows greeted him. Vines that looked as neat and organized as the ones on the neighboring property.

Kyle closed his eyes; surely tiredness was causing this hallucination. He opened them and the sight remained unchanged.

Was this why he'd been signing all those checks recently? Who gave permission to tend to the vines? He hadn't, that's for sure. What was happening here? What didn't he know about? But he bet Shey knew. If it weren't so late, he'd call her and ask what the hell was going on.

A yawn ripped through him. Tomorrow. He would sort it out tomorrow. With one last look, he doused the lights and made his way to his bedroom, shedding his trousers and tossing them into the laundry room as he passed. He should take a shower, but fatigue sank its claws into him.

Fighting off another yawn, he entered his bedroom and made his way to his bed. A thought tugged at the back of his mind, a thought that things weren't quite right in the house. A thought he should take notice of, but was too tired to try to understand.

Tomorrow everything would make sense.

• • •

Jordan Hastings washed the shampoo out of her hair while listing all the things she needed to do that day. There was nothing more invigorating than getting up as the sun rose out of the sky to begin a brand new day.

She needed to check and make sure the new shoots were growing straight, obtaining maximum sunshine on the budding fruit stock. She also needed to make sure there was no sign of mildew on the vines. After being neglected for so long, she wasn't expecting much from this year's harvest. With the grapes she did manage to grow and harvest, she hoped to experiment and come up with new blends, new flavors infused into the wines.

Jordan couldn't wait for her dad to recover from his broken leg so he could help her when it came to harvesting the grapes. Good thing she happened to be visiting him when he had his accident. She tried not to think his fall was caused by hearing about her broken engagement. Or how her former fiancé had won the Golden Wine award for "Most Innovative Wine" for the wine she'd created. She tried to convince herself none of those things was the reason her father lost his balance on the ladder, fell and broke his leg. But she couldn't help but feel responsible.

Jordan forcefully shut off the water. She wasn't going to think about her loser ex. The only important male person in her life was her father, and she planned to keep it that way for a long time. She wasn't going to be fooled by a handsome face again.

She shoved the shower curtain aside and screamed.

"...a short and sweet book about finding healing after a tragedy and letting love in." —4 stars, United Indie Book Blog

For more books by Nicole Flockton, check out:

Daniel's Decision

"This was a wonderful book of two people both following their dreams to the ends of the earth, and learning a valuable lesson along the way. I loved the character of Daniel so very much that the man had me in tears on a regular basis. Tears of frustration, joy, anger and hope . . . I am taking away a message of when we find love, we should not let our goals or perfect sea of life get in the way - sometimes you need to bend the rules a little to get what you want." -- 5 stars, Contemporary Romance Reviews

"Once again, Nicole Flockton has created a couple with a wonderful and immediate chemistry - one you can believe in. Another winner from the pen of Ms. Flockton!"—My Written Romance

"If you want a fun and entertaining read, don't miss Daniel's Decision by Nicole Flockton"— 4 stars, Harlequin Junkie
Masquerade

Rescuing Dawn

Seducing Phoebe

Praise for the Lovers Unmasked series:

"I just loved this story . . . If you like a good, fun and oh so sexy read, make sure you don't miss *Seducing Phoebe*." —Harlequin Junkie

"A fun and ultimately satisfactory read, this is the last of the series but can be read as a stand-alone book, and is certain to become a favorite of many."—I Am, Indeed

"I loved this book! There was angst and the return of an ex-boyfriend on the eve of the heroine's wedding to a man whose 'been there' for her all along."—Caribbean Accent Book Reviews

"This was my first time reading a book by Nicole Flockton and it will not be my last. If you enjoy a true romance book then this is the one for you!" —Tiffany Talks Books

"Flockton does a fabulous job of making Dawn's pain real and developing her as a multi-dimensional character. I felt horrible for Dawn, but I didn't pity her. I respected her for coming through such a devastating experience. There's often a fine line between writing a character that annoys readers and a character readers feel for. Flockton does a fabulous job here."—Shana Galen, RITA finalist and author of *If You Give a Rake a Ruby*

"An extremely emotional and sweet romance that will break your heart, make you cry and make you smile, don't miss *Rescuing Dawn* by Nicole Flockton."—Harlequin Junkie

In the mood for more Crimson Romance?
Check out *Sweet Texas Kiss by Monica Tillery* at
CrimsonRomance.com.